Voices

A
short story
collection

written by
Emi Sano

For inquiries, contact:
emisanowrites@gmail.com

Book and Cover design by Emi Sano
Edited by Emily Pierson

ISBN: 978-0-578-53659-0
First Edition:
10 9 8 7 6 5 4 3 2 1

To my husband,
for your love and patience
while I pursue my dream.

TABLE OF CONTENTS

FAMILY

HENRY HIGGINS

HENRY HIGGINS, AGE 82, INTROVERT.

Henry enjoyed the simple life. He did everything alone and he liked that. Nevertheless, his neighbors mistook his solitary life as loneliness and did everything they could to have him take part in social gatherings.

Henry did his best to please his neighbors by attending and sitting in a chair throughout the evenings, but he'd much rather sit in his chair at his home.

Adelaide was his next-door neighbor, she too, was 82 years old, but very extroverted.

Whenever she held a gathering, whether it was with family or friends, she was the life of the party. She always had the best jokes. Henry enjoyed listening to her talk amongst others. To Henry, she was the most liked in the neighborhood.

Adelaide always made a point to approach Henry whenever he attended. She made him feel important.

Henry never had any visitors. After he lost his wife, Henry's family continued on in their own lives. He knew they would be better off not hanging around a quiet old man. He was okay with that.

Then, an awful day happened. Adelaide had a heart attack and was rushed to the hospital. Everyone was worried about her, even Henry, but he avoided hanging around the crowd. Instead, Henry worried on his own, hoping Adelaide would come home and be his neighbor again soon.

Unfortunately, Adelaide died that evening. Henry watched as her family filed into her home, grieving. He, too, grieved that night.

Despite liking his alone time, Henry was saddened to have lost his only friend.

The next day, someone knocked on his door. Henry nervously answered. Adelaide's oldest daughter stood with a box of Henry's favorite chocolate.

"What's this?" Henry asked confused, then quickly added, "I'm very sorry for your loss."

Adelaide's daughter held back tears as she handed him the box.

"Me, too." She said, "Mom knew you liked these. She'd want you to have them so you wouldn't be too sad without her."

Henry took the box. "That's very kind of you. I, uh, didn't realize she knew that much about me."

Adelaide's daughter burst into tears.

"Papa, don't you even recognize me?" Henry took a step back. He shook his head. He didn't remember having a daughter, especially with Adelaide. "It's me, Gabby."

Gabby started crying more. "Papa, please, mom just died. We need you to come back to us."

Henry, frightened, staggered backwards into his home.

"I'm sorry, Gabby, even though my children haven't visited for quite some time, I'd remember if I had a daughter."

Gabby shook her head and reached into her pocket. She pulled out a picture of Adelaide in her thirties, with three small children and Henry holding the youngest. Henry looked at the picture in shock, but how could that be?

Suddenly, the memory of him fighting with Gabby as she told him she wasn't going to medical school like she planned, but getting married to a Navy man she met instead. This memory triggered something in his brain and suddenly it was like Henry was a different person.

Henry looked at Gabby with new eyes. He saw his daughter in tears. Very quickly, he wrapped her up in his arms like he used to whenever she got hurt.

"My darling, Gabriella, you're going to be quite all right. I'm here." Henry looked around and noticed his home was just a room. He felt afraid for a moment. "How long do I have?"

"Last time was only an hour... we wanted you to have a chance to say goodbye to Mom." Gabby said through tears. She tried to gather herself quickly. "We should go."

Henry nodded in understanding. He quickly followed her to the car. The ride was quiet, but both Gabby and Henry weren't bothered by the silence. You could say that Gabby took after Henry the most.

"We're going to cremate Mom and you can keep her ashes with you." Gabby said as they pulled up to the funeral home.

"Thank you, I would like that very much." Henry said as they made their way into the room where Adelaide was resting.

Along with Adelaide, two other people were in the room. George and Gemma greeted their father with hugs. Henry held them tightly and studied their faces, hoping he wouldn't forget them ever again.

"I'm so glad you're here, Papa." Gemma said as she laid her hand on his arm. She was the little one he held in the picture.

"Mom would've loved to know you came." George tried to smile, but he was too broken up.

George was Adelaide's favorite. She would never admit that, but Henry knew, and so did George.

Henry walked over to where Adelaide rested. He bent over so he could really study her face one last time.

Her laugh lines were etched into her face permanently. There was never a day where she didn't smile or laugh. Adelaide had these beautiful brown eyes that shot through your soul if you wronged her in any way. Her eyes were closed, but he could remember them, because his daughters shared the same eyes. Her smooth skin stretched across her cheekbones. Henry lightly touched them. Tears fell from his cheeks to hers.

How could he forget her, his best friend and only love? How could he not remember who she was this whole time?!

Henry kissed her forehead one last time before turning to his children.

"I'm sorry, for everything. All your pain, I wouldn't wish this on you, ever."

"Oh, Papa! We're not mad at you." Gemma said.

"Mom always invited you whenever we visited, but we had to act like you were just her friend. It was still good to see you." Gabby clarified. "She didn't want you to be alone, Papa. We won't let you be alone either."

"Thank you." Tears fell down Henry's cheeks some more. His children came together and gave him a group hug.

Before they left, Henry told his wife one last time, how much he loved her.

Gabby took him back home.

Henry thanked Adelaide's daughter for the chocolates. When she left, he returned to his chair. He ate his chocolate with a small feeling of nostalgia.

As the day grew into night, he heard his neighbors get together and wondered if Adelaide was joining them in spirit.

CHARLIE

CHARLIE LEANED BACK IN HER OFFICE CHAIR IN DEEP THOUGHT. She was struggling with putting down the words that would finish her essay that she had hoped to publish. Books by Ta-Nehisi Coates, Joan Didion, Ralph Waldo Emerson, and Virginia Woolf, sat on her bookshelf. All her favorite inspirational works sat, collecting dust, something she hoped this essay would do for someone else's bookshelf.

Is it strange that I want my own work collecting dust on someone's shelf? She thought as she attempted to figure out how to sum up her hard work. Charlie had been working on an essay on niche culture and how social media helps and hurts. She'd worked through a crazy amount of hours for research and gathering intel from countless experts. Sleepless nights contributed to her writing. You could say she put her blood, sweat, and tears into this body of work.

Now she was stuck. It was the last few pages of her essay and she couldn't figure out how to close it.

Frustrated, she slammed the laptop shut and got off the chair. She wasn't sure how long her body had been in that chair, but her stiff joints and painful movements indicated that it had been more than just a few hours.

She grabbed her smartphone that lay sadly on her desk and checked to see if there were any notifications. Unfortunately, there were several... all from her mother.

She decided that calling would be the best way to respond.

"Charlotte Anne! What the hell, I've been trying to contact you for hours!" Charlie cringed; her mother used her full name. She tried to wrap her head around her mother's sudden need to catch her.

"But, you didn't call me..."

"That's because I didn't think you'd answer."

Charlie reflected on that and agreed, "You're right. What's the matter? Where's the fire?"

"Charlie, it's your dad... He had to go the hospital. He's okay for now, but the doctors are running tests to find out what's going on." Charlie's heart stopped for a few milliseconds, she didn't hear the rest of what her mother said.

"I'm coming."

"Charlie, you're almost done with your essay..."

"I'm finished. I'm coming." Charlie lied as she started running into her bedroom to collect her belongings.

"Honey... I don't want you to come out here if this just happens to be a fluke thing."

"It's okay, I need a vacation after working on this for so long. I'll be there first thing in the morning. Love you, bye."

Charlie hung up the phone before her mother could say anything else. Her mind was racing. She knew she needed to finish that essay, but being with her father was more important. If she didn't go see him and something happened, she'd never finish that essay.

She ran back into her office and stuffed her laptop and its charger into her bag and out the door she went. Maybe she could get some writing done while at home.

It was going to be an all-nighter drive. Charlie lived four states away from her family. In retrospect, it wasn't the best decision to move out to New York, but she thought she'd have more inspiration and a better chance of landing a publisher if she lived closer to them.

Her father never understood why she majored in sociology and cultural anthropology, believing those degrees wouldn't make any money and she'd be stuck teaching. Her father wanted Charlie to excel in life and live better than they did.

Charlie had to prove to him that being a sociologist was so much more than teaching.

She yearned to write essays and journals to help improve and change the societal discourse that's been happening as of late. When she wrote her thesis paper for her master's degree on mob mentality and it was published in her professor's online journal, her father finally softened on his idea of her career path.

Everything she worked for was all thanks to her father. He was just a simple manufacturing technician, it being the only job he could get out of high school. He always spoke to Charlie about work and the people he worked with. He would complain about his bosses and wondered why they never listen to him or his other coworkers whenever an issue arose. He would voice, "If I could just get into their heads to understand."

Charlie would sit and listen, because what else can you do as a little girl? She was curious, too. But she wasn't really interested in getting inside his bosses' head. She was more interested in the environment he worked at and the mentality behind his bosses and coworkers. Why was there an established divide? Who decided that the bosses would always be right?

By the time she was in high school, she discovered sociology and from then on she pursued that path, much to her father's dismay. He really wanted her to be a lawyer. Charlie was always very skilled at debates and he felt that her talents would be lost if she kept going down the humanities route. But she proved him wrong and he was once again flabbergasted about how brilliant his daughter came to be.

As Charlie neared hour six of her nine-hour trip she knew she needed to take a break. But, it was nearly eleven o'clock at night and not a lot of places would be open.

"I just need to get coffee," she said out loud. Hearing her voice actually caused her to jump. She hadn't realized she'd been driving in total silence for the past two hours when her Pandora station stopped playing.

She decided to pull into a Waffle House, because those places were always open and getting something to eat wouldn't be so bad either. Her stomach growled as she turned off the car.

When was the last time I ate?

She checked her messages to see if her mother had left any news, but so far it'd been radio silent. Charlie texted her mother, but no response meant either her mother was too preoccupied with worrying over her husband or she went to sleep because she couldn't handle staying awake. Charlie always said her mother was an anxiety sleeper. Whenever something made her mother anxious it would put her right to sleep. That was how she coped. For Charlie, if she were anxious, she would be up for a week.

For the rest of the drive, Charlie reflected on her time spent with her father. She was already preparing for him to leave her even though her mother mentioned several times that he was okay, for now. Charlie knew that her mother tended to underreact in severe situations.

One instance was when Charlie had broken her arm playing outside with her friends. Charlie couldn't look at her arm because she was in so much pain and her mother, the nurse, just told her it's fine; it was just a minor break. It was broken in three places.

Charlie remembered one time when her father came home after injuring himself at work. He was in so much pain, but he had to go back to work the next day. She remembered her mother telling him to take the day off and rest, but he insisted that he go back. He never asked for workman's compensation. He just returned to work, persevered, and finished out the week.

That weekend they were supposed to go the batting cages so Charlie could practice her softball swing. Her father looked so defeated when he told her they couldn't go. Charlie didn't cry or put up a fight. She understood and spent the weekend by his side, reading her books. She wasn't sure if he enjoyed her commentary on what she was learning about, or if he was even listening, but she did enjoy that entire weekend of just the two of them, learning together.

She neared the final stretch to her home. She saw the signs pointed for her town and her heart began to pound. She looked at her phone again for any signs from her mother and she got nothing. As she rolled up to her family home, the tires kicking up gravel, she felt a sense of nostalgia. Everything looked the same as it did when she was ten years old.

She entered her home to find it empty and dark. Her mother must have stayed the night at the hospital. Charlie made her way into the living room and crashed on the couch. She couldn't bring herself up the stairs to her bedroom... she was too tired and too emotionally drained.

In the morning, she felt a soft touch through her hair. She jostled awake to find a blanket had been laid over her and her mother was sitting beside her.

"How's Dad?" Charlie asked as she pulled herself away from sleep.

"You know, he's a fighter."

"Is it bad? What happened? You didn't even tell me."

"I did. You hung up when I was explaining... he had a cardiac arrest. It wasn't too severe. They were able to revive him quickly."

"So?"

"They think it's something else that caused it."

Charlie tried to swallow, but her mouth was dry.

"What do you mean?"

"I don't know, Charlie... they think he might be low on some levels. It wasn't heart disease."

"You're a nurse, mom."

"I'm not a doctor."

Charlie's mother broke down into tears. Charlie got up and hugged her mom tightly.

"He looked so vulnerable when they were reviving him. I panicked, Charlie."

"He's awake now, though, right?"

"Yes, I told him you were coming, so get changed and we'll head over."

Charlie nodded and quickly pulled out some clothes from her bag. She wasn't sure what she even packed, and immediately regretted packing so quickly. None of her clothes matched or even was okay to wear to a hospital.

Emi Sano

Oh well, Dad doesn't care if I'm in sweats.
Charlie shrugged on her yoga tank and met her
mother out in the car.

Her mother raised her eyebrows at
Charlie's outfit but didn't say a word.

"I packed blindly."

They rode to the hospital in silence. It was
her mother's silence that worried Charlie the
most. She was always filled with trivial small
talk, because her mother hated those awkward
lulls in conversation. Charlie picked up that
habit and it always made her the "weird" girl in
school.

"So, how's work?" Charlie asked.

"Good. They're slowly cutting down my
hours because I'm going to retire in a few years.
They want the other nurses to be able to fill my
shoes."

"Oh... but are you getting paid enough still?"

"Oh yeah! I'm finally working a 40-hour
workweek! It's been fantastic." Charlie's
mother smiled genuinely. She pulled up into
the hospital parking lot. "They gave me some
time off to stay with your dad, but I've been
sort of micromanaging the nurses here."

"Mom!"

"I know, and they listen to me because I'm still their boss." Charlie's mother face-palmed. "I'm really bad."

"Well, let's hope Dad gets out soon otherwise you might not have a job to go back to."

They both laughed as they got out of the car. *Back to normal*, Charlie hoped.

Standing in the doorway to his room, Charlie could see her father lay helplessly on the hospital bed. His normally large presence felt small inside this room. It saddened Charlie to see him so weak. He was already awake when they walked in.

Charlie came over to the bed and took his hand. If you looked at Charlie's family photo, you would think Charlie's father was adopted. He had darker hair, darker skin, and darker eyes than both her mother and Charlie. He was part Japanese and European, and Charlie's mother was all European... so naturally Charlie came out looking like a Swedish model. Except for her eyes. She had brown eyes shaped like her father. Nobody could ever place where Charlie came from.

"Hey Dad."

"Hey Charlie. How's the writing going?"

"Good, I'm pretty much finished."

"You didn't have to come all the way down here."

"Of course I did."

Just then, Marcie, Charlie's mother's co-worker and father's doctor walked in with the chart along with Charlie's mother looking over it.

"Hey Charlotte, I didn't know you were here!" Marcie gave Charlie a hug.

"Hi Marcie – Dr. Carson."

"Oh, quiet with that professional crap. How's my favorite sociologist doing?"

"Just finishing my second essay."

"She's going to change the world, Marcie." Charlie's father interjected. Charlie gave her father a little push to shut up. Marcie laughed as she started looking over the chart again.

"Okay, *Mr. Akko*, looks like your tests are back. You want to know what happened?"

Marcie pulled the chart away from Charlie's mother's line of sight with a smile.

"Sure, doc, lay it on me."

"Well, you've been dealing with a lot of stress haven't you? Your blood pressure was really high, and on top of that you have low levels of potassium... Sarah says you haven't been eating right lately, is that right?" Marcie eyed Charlie's mother.

"Yeah, I've been working late shifts, trying to train the new kids."

"I see. Well, it's no surprise then, you had a very minor heart attack. You can go home tomorrow." Marcie signed off on the chart and handed it to Charlie's mother. "Get him on a better diet. I don't want to see you back in here again, Steven."

Charlie's father and mother both nodded with relief.

"I told you, Char," her father said with a smile.

"It's okay, I need a break. Is it all right that I stay a few more days?"

"You can stay forever," Charlie's mother said while laughing.

"Charlotte, I'd love to hear about your essay while you're here!" Marcie said as she walked out the room.

Charlie stayed for a few more days. She spent time talking to her father about her essay. She finally revealed that she's been stuck on the last chapter for days.

"It's okay. It's not like you're on a deadline."

"Yeah, just you know, my career depends on this."

"You got to live life a little to get experience! Nothing worth writing about will be in the books, because someone has already written about it!" Charlie's father's words resonated with her. She hadn't really thought about it like that.

"Why have you stayed with this job, after all these years? Why not change?"

"Are you analyzing me?"

"I'm not a psychologist, Dad."

"I don't know. To be honest, after being here for a while I felt like my bosses understood me, and nobody ever complained about my work. So, why change?"

"But it's been a strain on you for as long as I remember."

"Yeah, but it's the only work I know how to do."

Charlie nodded. "So, in a way, you found your niche and were too afraid to branch out."

"I knew you were analyzing me." Charlie's father cracked a smile.

Charlie was afraid to go back to her apartment, but she knew that finishing the essay would be easier. Even though her father didn't go to college or earned a degree in sociology, he was always filled with insight and wisdom that she couldn't learn in school.

When she said her goodbyes before hitting the road she gave her father an extra long hug.

"Please don't scare me like that again."

"Scout's honor."

"You weren't in the scouts."

"Shut up and go finish that essay." Charlie's father pushed her towards the car. He waved her off as she pulled out of her childhood home.

Even if the trip originated on terrible circumstances, she was glad she came down.

Everything is going to be okay, Charlie thought as she turned on her favorite Pandora station and entered the highway.

When she returned home, Charlie sat in her office chair and finished her essay.

SAMMIE

"I THINK YOU'RE OVERREACTING," Darryl said as he picked up his phone to read his emails.

Sammie sat on the other end of the couch feeling a bit unheard. She stared at Darryl for a few more seconds before getting off the couch and leaving the room.

This was the first time she felt her feelings invalidated by her husband. He was always calling it as he felt, but he normally sided with her or at least validated her fears whenever she brought them up. But tonight, he didn't.

Overreacting, she thought, *I'll show you overreacting*.

Sammie plopped herself onto her bed. She couldn't shut her mind off on what was plaguing her. She was worried that her little attitude outburst at work would cause her to lose her job. She always kept a level head about her and wasn't sure how her boss took that outburst. She ran out of the office before she could find out. It was embarrassing and she didn't have a reason for it to escalate that way.

Today was just a terrible day to begin with. Her coffee spilt everywhere and she was late to work because of it. All of her projects contained some aspect that went wrong when it was supposed to go smoothly. She did the math; there should have been no bumps in production. But it felt like everyone was calling her today with a problem that needed to be fixed, right then and there.

And then her boss came up to her and commented on how her performance today at the meeting wasn't her best.

"I don't give a flying fuck if it wasn't its best. I did my best," Sammie snapped. It was like someone had possessed her for those few seconds. The whole office floor was silent. Sammie looked around and saw that everyone was looking at her from over their cubicle walls. She felt claustrophobic and wanted to flee. She looked at her boss whose lips were pursed.

When she relayed her fears about being fired to her husband, he didn't think it was a big deal to worry over. That didn't make Sammie feel any better than she did on the drive home.

Darryl came into the bedroom and saw Sammie, still plopped on the bed in the same position she was in when she first got on. He sighed and crawled into bed with her. He wrapped his arms around her waist and pulled her in tightly against his body.

"I know you're worried, but I think if you just calmly explain to your boss, she'll understand. We all have those days. Don't need to stress about it."

Sammie started to cry. Darryl hugged tighter.

"I must have fit the angry black woman stereotype."

"I'm sure you felt like Viola out there, didn't you?" Darryl chuckled behind Sammie.

Sammie felt a smile creep through her lips. She turned around to look at Darryl. His face always soothed her. His deep warm brown eyes always melted away any trouble.

"Thanks, baby." Sammie kissed his lips sweetly.

"I'm sorry I made you feel worse."

"No, I just didn't hear what I wanted. You're right, I'm overreacting."

Darryl smirked. He put his lips against Sammie's forehead. She melted into his warm body. Just like that, her fears went away.

The next day at work, Sammie cautiously walked into the office. She avoided any eye contact with her coworkers as she made her way to her desk.

"Sammie!"

Sammie paused hearing her name and winced when she realized it was her boss. She turned around to face her. A huge smile was plastered on her boss' face. Sammie felt like she walked into the Stepford Wives.

"Care to talk in my office?" her boss asked, still smiling.

Sammie nodded in response and followed her boss into her office.

"Listen, Katie, I can explain..."

"No, it's fine. I reflected after you left and I'm not even that mad you said that. It's true, you did your best and that's what I should have said."

"I just had a really bad day yesterday. It won't happen again."

"We all get bad days... even myself. I think I projected that on you as well. Care to forget it ever happened?"

Sammie couldn't believe her ears, but she nodded anyway. "Yeah, sure. See you at the two o'clock."

Sammie left Katie's office feeling like a weight has lifted off her chest. She couldn't believe that it actually happened.

"So, did you get fired?" Justin, her best friend and coworker, asked during the lunch break.

"Would I be eating lunch if I did?"

"True. Well that was some outburst, girl. I didn't even know you had it in you."

"Me neither." Sammie stabbed at her salad. "I'm still in shock I didn't get written up."

"I heard that Nicole was going to call security..." Justin watched Sammie's reaction before continuing, "that racist bitch."

Sammie chuckled. Nicole had always been trying to find ways to get Sammie fired from the office ever since Sammie started working.

"She can't even figure out how to use the security speed dial. I think I'll be okay." Sammie responded.

Justin howled in laughter. He clutched his stomach, he was laughing so hard. Sammie laughed along with him.

"Where were you yesterday when I needed this laugh?" Sammie glared at Justin.

"Sorry, I was too busy kissing Frank's ass for a promotion."

"Did it work?"

"Girl, would I be sitting in here with you if it did?" They laughed some more.

The rest of the day Sammie felt uneasy. She couldn't shake that nagging feeling that something was going to go wrong. She knew that her boss was willing to put it behind her. So why couldn't she?

When Sammie got home she was only greeted by her retired K9 German Shepherd, Zane.

"Where's Daddy, Zane?"

Zane ran around in circles, just excited for someone to be home. It wasn't normal for Darryl to be home from work later than Sammie. Since Zane retired, they changed their schedules so that he wouldn't be left alone for too long.

Sammie checked her phone for any messages she might have missed, but there was nothing. So, she called Darryl.

"Hey this is Darryl, leave a message!" The voicemail message was followed by a BEEP.

"Darryl, it's me. Just checking where you are... thought you said you'd be out earlier today. Call me back." Sammie ended her call. That dark, dreadful feeling was growing inside of her. Something was wrong... but it wasn't with her job.

Sammie tried to take her mind off it by taking Zane out for a long walk around the neighborhood. She felt maybe the walk might lead her to Darryl. Maybe he was out for a jog and he didn't want to bring Zane or his phone with him.

All sorts of thoughts flooded Sammie's mind. The walk wasn't helping and she was getting extremely frustrated with Zane as he kept stopping to smell every blade of grass they walked past. She could feel the heat rise in her cheeks as her eyes started to water.

Something was wrong. *Something was wrong.*

Sammie turned around the corner to her street and noticed a few cop cars sitting outside her house. She immediately felt a ball drop in the pit of her stomach. Something... was... wrong.

She didn't know how, but her feet carried her to her front yard where she met the officers who were standing in idle waiting for Sammie to arrive. She recognized one of them, Officer Samuels, but she stayed inside her car. Sammie tried to wave at her, but Officer Samuels avoided eye contact. This was a bad sign.

"Mrs. Livingston?" Another officer asked as she approached.

"It's actually Sammie Ellings, I didn't change my last name when we married."

The officer nodded and took off the hat he was wearing. He ran his fingers through his hair trying to find the words.

"Your husband was involved in an accident," he finally said.

Sammie took a deep breath. This was a part of his job description, that he would be put in harm's way every day. She knew this.

"What kind of accident?" Sammie tried to not break down into tears before she could find out more information. "Is he okay?"

"He is in the hospital. There was a shoot-out during one of his stops. One of the K9's at the scene saved him."

Zane whined, he didn't like being in one spot for too long and the sight of the cop car made him anxious to get to work. Sammie put her hand on his head and slowly patted him while she processed this information.

"Is he conscious?"

"For a few moments. He told us to get you."

Sammie walked over to Officer Samuels' window and banged on it for her to open.

"What's wrong? Why can't you look me in the eye, Samuels? What happened?"

Officer Samuels refused to look at Sammie.

"What aren't you telling me?!?"

Zane started to bark, feeding off his owner's anxiety.

"Ma'am, please, let's just put your dog back into the house and we can take you to him."

Sammie reigned Zane in with his leash and held him close.

"I'm not leaving him. He can come with... he's a retired K9 doesn't that give him some special clearance?"

"I'm afraid not. Unless he was a support animal, which he wasn't trained for."

"Bullshit! He's a fucking K9!"

"Sammie..." Officer Samuels was getting out of the car. "Sammie, please, we really need to get you to the hospital. Just put Zane back in the house."

Sammie felt her anxiety wash over again.

This is not happening! She exclaimed in her head. She felt like screaming.

Once again, Sammie moved towards the house, not really sure how she did it, but she put Zane back into the house and put down food and water for him. She wasn't sure how long she'd be. She grabbed his favorite puzzle toy and put in treats for him to find while she was walking out.

In the cop car, everyone was silent. She learned the officer that spoke with her first was named Owen Johnson. He was green and Samuels' new partner. He elected to sit in the back so Sammie could feel comfortable.

Samuels drove in silence. Every time Sammie looked at her, she wouldn't return a glance.

"What aren't you telling me?"

"I can't tell you anything." Officer Samuels finally spoke as they approached the hospital. "They'll tell you when you get in."

Sammie entered the hospital in a daze. She felt as if she had left her body and someone else was controlling it. Another officer was ready to escort her to Darryl's room. She could feel her feet move forward, but her brain was in a fog. Her heart was beating so fast, it felt slow. The blood was pumping in her ears, all she could hear was the whooshing noise it made. The officer tried to make small talk with Sammie, but she didn't hear any of it.

Woosh. Woosh. Sammie stepped into the room where Darryl was set up. He had tubes and wires coming out of him. Everything was plugged into a machine that was keeping him alive.

Sammie immediately ran to Darryl's side. His eyes were closed. A machine was helping him breathe. She took his hand and it felt cool.

"Is he dying?" Sammie looked up at the nurse who was checking the monitors. The nurse looked at Sammie and shook her head.

"I'll go get the doctor and let her explain." She tried to smile at Sammie before walking out.

Dr. Lee Han walked in carrying a tablet, reading the screen. She looked up and saw Sammie, distraught and waiting for any answers.

"We put him an induced coma. His brain experienced extreme trauma and we're giving him time to heal. We already put him through surgery and took out all the bullets. There were five total."

Five? Sammie put her face in her hands. "Will he be okay?"

"Time will tell." Dr. Lee walked over to Sammie. She placed her hand on Sammie's shoulder. "I'm sorry we didn't get to ask you if we can induce the coma, it was a matter of life and death."

Sammie shook her head, "It's okay. I'm glad you guys did everything you can. How long will he be like this?"

"Days, weeks? We're hoping days. He just needs to heal." Dr. Lee went to walk away but Sammie stopped her.

"Thank you."

Dr. Lee nodded and walked out of the room.

Sammie found a chair and sat beside Darryl's bed. She grabbed a hold of his hand again and squeezed it tight. He looked so vulnerable... so weak. At six foot two, under all those tubes and wires... it was the first time she's ever seen him so small.

Sammie called Katie to let her know that she wasn't going into work the next few days. Katie was extremely empathetic and told her to take as much time as she needed.

Her next call was to Darryl's family. Although they were only married for a few years it felt like his family had been with her all her life. They only lived a few hours away.

Darryl's mama was distraught at first hearing her child was in the hospital but she immediately turned into mama mode and assured Sammie that they will be there soon and not to worry about Zane or anything at home.

Sammie then called her mom who lived across the country. She announced that she was going to catch the next flight even though Sammie told her to wait and that she would be in good company soon. Her mother wasn't listening and said she'd be on the plane tomorrow.

It was funny, Sammie was going to be surrounded by her whole family, but she never felt so alone. Darryl was her everything and if she were to lose him, she would lose her life.

Somehow Darryl's parents came in record time. They even had Zane with them and hollered their way into the hospital room with the dog. Sammie could hear Darryl's mama down the hall.

"HE IS A DECORATED AND RETIRED K9 OFFICER. HE IS NO DOG."

Darryl's mama huffed her way into the room and Zane came barreling through behind her out of the grasp of Darryl's father's hands. He looked at Sammie and shrugged.

Sammie took a hold of Zane who was ecstatic to see his mom. Zane quickly sniffed at the bed Darryl was on and then whined. "It's okay, Daddy's just sleeping. Lay down." Sammie said to Zane who obediently obeyed her command. "Did they really let you come through?"

"You mean you didn't hear her?" Darryl's father chuckled as he took a seat in another chair.

Darryl's mama was already at Darryl's other side checking his vitals, not believing the machines. She used to be a nurse until she retired last year.

"Yeah, I did, I just thought they were going to end up throwing y'all out."

"Child, they cannot throw out the mama of an officer of the law! Especially if he's in the hospital after doing God's work. That's injustice." Darryl's mama softly caressed Darryl's cheek and then joined her husband's side. "How are you holding up, dear? Do you need to go home?"

"I don't want to leave him."

"Oh, honey, I assure you these doctors are doing everything they can to keep him alive. His heart rate is steady."

"They wouldn't really tell me all that happened. Just that he got hit five times." Sammie shook her head and petted Zane. He looked up at Sammie and whined again.

"I think you should go home and just rest. Have you eaten dinner?"

"No. What time is it?"

"Don't you worry. We will take you home and whip something up for you, won't we Damien?"

Darryl's father nodded and stood up, "Let's go, Sammie-girl, before the hospital goes nuts with Zane being here."

Sammie got up and convinced Zane to follow her out the room. Zane didn't want to leave Darryl's side. Sammie felt the same.

At home, Sammie sat on the very couch she sat on last night when she had her talk with Darryl. It felt weird to her, that it only happened last night. She thought it was last week. Time had become an unfamiliar concept to Sammie. What time was it now?

Sammie looked at her phone and saw that it was almost ten o'clock. Was it still the same day? Her mind was wandering to different scenarios about her future.

They didn't get the chance to have kids. They were waiting until this year to start trying. Darryl wanted to build up his savings before they had any kids and Sammie did as well. They had just enough to be able to afford any emergencies and were going to celebrate that this weekend. The emergency came earlier than expected.

Sammie refused to think their future was about to be cut by Fate's scissors. She willed herself to think that he would survive and their dreams would continue to flourish. Sammie wasn't left alone to her thoughts for long. Darryl's mama came into the room and did everything in the book to keep her mind from wandering. Sammie knew where Darryl got his strength and calm demeanor from and she so wished she could be just like that for him.

"My mom should be flying in by the morning." Sammie told Darryl's mama.

"We'll get her when she comes in. Come on, let's get you to bed, baby. We'll get up in the morning to see him. Damien will be there tonight."

Sammie felt her body stand up and make its way to the bedroom. She climbed into bed with Zane and tried to go to sleep. But with Darryl's mama gone, her thoughts came flooding back and she couldn't shut them off. By the time morning came, she saw the sun peak through the blinds.

Sammie's mother was the second thing she saw that morning. Her softened demeanor almost scared Sammie. She'd never seen her mother as vulnerable as she was.

"How's baby doing?"

"She's feeling shitty."

Sammie's mother chuckled a little and that softened demeanor went away as she whipped Sammie in to shape to go to the hospital.

At the hospital, Darryl was still hooked up to everything. Sammie wanted to rip it all out so she could get to his face. It was hard not to be able to look into his eyes and feel his warm embrace. She just wanted him to smile at her and tell her everything was going to be okay. But right now that smile was covered by the breathing machine.

Her anxiety levels rose as Dr. Lee came in. Sammie couldn't make her hands stop shaking.

"Are you okay, Ms. Ellings?"

Sammie could barely hear what Dr. Lee was saying. That fog filled her head and she suddenly found herself falling to the floor.

A whole range of commotion happened at once.

She heard her mother scream.

Dr. Lee checked for a pulse and yelled for help.

Nurses flew into the room as Dr. Lee barked a ton of orders and Sammie was suddenly hooked up to an IV and was receiving oxygen from a mask. When she finally came to, Sammie was lying in a bed beside Darryl and stuck in a daze.

Darryl was no longer hooked up to a thousand tubes and wires. Just the one heart monitor and an IV. Sammie couldn't believe her eyes that she was looking at the warm brown eyes she had longed for.

"He heard us yelling... and came to." Sammie's mother told her as Sammie finally woke up from the grogginess.

"Fell back asleep and scared us all to death, but he woke up in time for you to wake up." Darryl's mama chuckled.

Darryl rolled his eyes, but he couldn't speak.

"Cat's got your tongue, baby?" Sammie asked Darryl.

He nodded.

"It's okay, your mama has enough words to speak for all of us." Sammie chuckled as Darryl's mama feigned offense.

Darryl's deep laugh registered and then he coughed and winced in pain.

"Sorry, baby. I shouldn't have made you laugh. I'm better now, you can keep resting." Sammie smiled as Darryl took a big deep breath and exhaled. He closed his eyes.

"Dr. Lee said you had a panic attack."

"That's what that was? I thought I was dying."

"She said you were harboring a lot of stress. Sweetie, you need to release some of that energy! It's not good for you to hold everything in." Sammie's mother was smoothing out Sammie's hair.

Sammie nodded, she knew that it was bad for her, but she didn't really think anyone would want to hear her problems. Sammie's mother gave her a prescription form with a name written on it. She told her that Dr. Lee had recommended the best therapist in the region and she better go see her.

"Yes, mom."

It was miraculous to Sammie, that Darryl had survived the whole ordeal with only a slight processing delay. Darryl was able to walk, talk, and joke around by the end of the second week in the hospital. All of her fears that she was holding inside her mind seemed to have been washed away after her panic attack. It was strange. She hadn't thought she would ever feel that calm again.

A month later, Sammie started seeing the therapist to talk about her anxiety. She learned that she was really experiencing something and it wasn't all in her head. Her therapist helped her with coping skills so if she ever felt another attack coming, she could stop it or put herself in a position where she could handle the attack better. It was like a weight had lifted from her shoulders. Most of her adult life she's struggled with her "irrational" fears. A lot of it had to do with Darryl's line of work and another was the way she worried about how she was perceived by other people. She learned how much worrying about what other people thought of her was affecting her body.

To have her anxiety validated by not only a therapist but her husband as well, made her feel confident enough to battle it head on.

"This battle isn't for the weakhearted," her therapist said one day. "You have to constantly be on the ready. When you finally win, you'll feel like a whole new person. I guarantee it. And I don't make many guarantees in my profession."

"If you say so." Sammie said with a nervous smile. She hated the idea of battling herself, but was enamored with the idea of being a new person. Someone confident and not scared of anything. Someone who could tell her boss to "fuck off" and not feel worried she'd lose her job.

For the record, Sammie has not told her boss to "fuck off" and has done her best not to test out that confidence theory.

CELIA

INSIDE A SMALL COTTAGE HOME LIVED AN OLD WOMAN NAMED CELIA WHO SPENT MOST OF HER DAYS TENDING TO HER GARDEN. Like most days, her routine was simple. In the morning, Celia would drink her coffee with a slice of buttered toast. After her breakfast, she would head outside while it was still cool to check her garden. The rest of the day consisted of busying herself in front of the television and knitting her great grandchildren sweaters.

Celia's been alone for six years now, since her husband unexpectedly fell ill. Her children begged her to sell the cottage and move in with one of them. She refused, feeling confident in being able to take care of herself. Her oldest child would stop by every week with her two grandkids.

"I'd like it better if you stayed with us, Mom. I worry about you out here," Hannah would say every time.

"As long as my flowers need me, I'm staying," Celia would insist. Unfortunately for Celia, Hannah was as stubborn as she. Hannah's relentless begging weighed heavily on her. She didn't want to cause worry on her children, but she also didn't want to be a burden in their household.

When her husband fell ill, it was chaos. All three children came and stayed at the house, each taking turns caring for him. She hated seeing him so helpless and didn't want her children's last days with him to be like that. Since then, Celia vowed that her kids would only see her best self. She decided she would move herself into hospice should she need it.

Celia confided in her youngest, Maxwell, about it. He wasn't happy about her eventually going into hospice, and of course told his older sisters. Hannah and Gillian came over at once to take her out of that mindset. She lied to them and said she would let them take care of her when the time came.

One day, while working on her garden, she felt a pain in her chest. *I'm old*, she thought to herself, *it's nothing to be alarmed about*. But later on, she was having trouble breathing. When this happened, she knew it was a heart attack. Maxwell was the closest to her, so she gave him a call. He immediately picked her up and took her to the ER. The doctor said she was lucky they caught it early enough. Maxwell said they were lucky he was working from home that day.

After she was discharged from the hospital she was brought to her second daughter, Gillian's home. She was the only one who could stay home with Celia every day.

But Celia just wanted to go to her home. Her flowers hadn't been tended to in a couple days and she worried the wildlife had taken notice. Of course, as much as she asked to go home, the longer she had to stay. Gillian promised they'd get someone to water her garden.

But what Gillian didn't understand was that Celia's garden was like her children. She wanted to be the one to nurture and take care of them... not a stranger. By the end of the week of being at Gillian's, she insisted that she be taken to her home at once.

Gillian caved in and took her mother to the cottage.

There was a young man already watering the garden when they arrived. Celia felt a fire burn inside her chest as the car rolled to a stop.

"You hired someone to take care of my garden?" Celia asked Gillian, trying not to sound too angry.

"I didn't want to, but Hannah insisted. She already had someone lined up. I'm sorry." Gillian sighed as she turned off the car.

Celia didn't respond, she got out of the car as fast as her body could let her and she hurried her legs over to where the man was finishing up the watering.

"Did you make sure to pull out the weeds before you watered?"

"Yes, ma'am."

"And checked them for damages from bugs and other wildlife?"

"Yes, ma'am. And trimmed some areas where it started to die." The gardener put down the hose and took off his gardening gloves. He extended out his hand for Celia to take. "I'm James. I work with your daughter's landscaper from time to time."

"Well, thank you for taking care of my garden while I was gone. I'm sure you have other gardens to work on. I can handle it from now on." Celia gripped James' hand as tight as she could for a quick shake before releasing.

"Mom!" Gillian was ashamed of her mother's rudeness. "He's just helping out until you're better. The doctor said you needed two weeks!"

"I'm fine, Gillian. Just let me move back home. This is my garden. I will not have someone else touch it as long as I'm alive. You hear me?" Celia was facing Gillian now with so much fierceness that you wouldn't have known she had a heart attack a week ago.

"If you don't mind, ma'am, I could just come by and help with the lifting of equipment and you can do all the work. Just to keep your daughters' minds at ease. Does that sound fair?" James proposed.

Gillian answered for Celia and agreed to those terms. She wouldn't let Celia get another word into the conversation and thanked James as he left.

Celia was fuming. She wasn't a child and she didn't need to be watched over like one either. So she had a heart attack. It was minor. She didn't need to have surgery. All she had to do was watch her blood pressure. To Celia, she was as fit as a horse.

After a few choice words at Gillian, her daughter left the house. Celia was proud of herself. She still held the mom power and she wasn't going to let it go easily.

Celia had forgotten that James was supposed to come by the next day and when he showed up, she was caught off guard. She almost clonked him with her watering can.

"Ma'am, I hope I'm not too late," James said, looking a bit embarrassed about the whole situation.

"No, you're right on time. If you want to help me, you'd grab that garden hose over there and get it unstuck. I couldn't move it so I'm stuck using this watering can today." Celia put James to work. The hose wasn't really stuck by accident. Celia actually made it that way on purpose after James and Gillian had left the cottage. If James were going to come by every day to "help" she'd rather make him feel useful by "fixing" things.

Celia continued with her gardening shift by tending to her perennials. They were close to blooming and she couldn't wait. They only stuck around for a short period of time, but seeing them bloom was the highlight of her year. She was worried that she was going to miss it if she stayed with Gillian any longer.

Each year she'd cut a couple before they die and let them live in her house for a few more days in the ceramic vase her husband bought her for Christmas. She chose different ones each year, but her favorite was the tulips. Celia loved how the bright colors lit up her kitchen, how their sweet, clean smell filled the air. They brought the kitchen to life.

James finished fixing the hose area by the time Celia was done with her gardening. She motioned for him to come inside while she made some iced tea. James was appreciative about the tea, but he was very ashamed that he didn't do much gardening work with Celia. She told him that it was quite all right and she was just glad that tomorrow she didn't have to use the watering can.

For the rest of the week, Celia had a to-do list for James to "fix" while she worked on different parts of her garden. She hoped that he wouldn't catch on to her antics, but if he had, he never let on that he knew.

Celia started to feel excited when James was going to come by. It was like she enjoyed having his company... even if he was just around to make sure she was still alive. After every "shift" they would come in and talk over iced tea. It was nice to have someone to talk to every day; Celia had almost forgotten what it was like.

By the second week, Celia started to allow James to help with the gardening. He had made a couple comments and suggestions about keeping the bugs off and the wildlife away from her vegetables. He brought some material to build around her tomatoes and she was grateful to see them untouched the next day.

Celia slowly trusted James with her garden. She could see that he was treating them just like she did... like they were his children. Although it was a strange feeling to see him talk to her flowers the way she did, she realized it was also a relief. Maybe she could leave the cottage after all. But it would only be to James.

"Are you looking to buy a home?" Celia asked James while they had their iced tea. James was taken aback for a second and nodded.

"Yes, actually, my wife and I just had our second child. We were thinking of getting a bigger home."

"Would you like to live in this one?"

James smiled bashfully and looked at her for a moment, trying to decide if she was serious. "I couldn't..."

"Well, James, I'm getting older by the day. And I don't want to sell this house to just anyone who's going to let my garden die. If I had to sell this house... it would be to you." Celia wasn't looking at James as she spoke. Her voice faltered. She didn't want to sell the home, but she was worried what would come of it when the time came and her children had to sell it for her.

"Ma'am... where would you live?"

"I'd move in with Hannah. She's the one that keeps insisting to move in with her anyway. I already have a bed there." Celia tried to smile to put James at ease.

James told her he would talk it over with his wife. Celia told him to come up with a price and she'll match it. She didn't care about making money from her home; all she cared about was the new owner taking great care of her garden.

It took a bit more convincing on Celia's part to get James to really consider buying the house. Celia could feel with each week passing, her body wasn't getting back the strength it used to have before the heart attack. She hated to admit that she really was getting old.

Her perennials had already gone away when James brought his wife and kids along to look at the house. One tulip managed to stay alive in her vase as it sat on the kitchen table.

"James, this place is magical." James' wife said to him as they looked through each room.

"My husband built everything in this house. He was a real craftsman." Celia boasted about the house's history. Distant memories came to mind of all the work that got put into this house and all the moments of their lives it encompassed. A part of her had a strong urge to push everyone out of the house so she could keep the memories in her life forever.

But she knew that it wouldn't have lasted long anyway.

Hannah was delighted to know that her mom finally made the decision to sell the house. She also knew how hard it was on Celia to do it, so she didn't show her excitement too much. Hannah made sure the house was prepared to have Celia and even had her landscaper prepare a small garden area for Celia to work on.

Celia was grateful for her daughter's actions. She never thought about starting a new garden when she left the cottage.

All of Celia's belongings were either sold or put into the basement of Hannah's house. Her son-in-law built extra shelves to put her most treasured items and swore that they will be safe there. The only thing Celia wanted to keep out of the basement was that ceramic vase.

It took awhile for Celia to get set in her new routine, which started with eating breakfast with her great grandchildren whom Hannah baby-sat for her eldest daughter, Leigh. She continued her regular day by gardening and teaching her great grandchildren all about the proper way of tending a garden. By the afternoon, she was sitting in front of the television Hannah set up for her in their former den. Hannah made sure to remodel that room into a Celia-approved living room – fit with her own furniture from the cottage.

Emi Sano

Celia sat in her usual chair watching the television as she knitted more clothes for her great grandchildren. She looked out the window and was able to see her little garden from where she sat. She swore she could see a tiny sprouting seed breaking its way through the soil.

Celia smiled. She was thankful to live another day to see a new generation grow.

REY

LIGHTS FLICKERED ANNOYINGLY AS REY SAT IN THE WAITING AREA. She stared at the ceiling watching them. She counted the seconds between each flicker. Ten seconds the first time, four seconds the next. It wasn't as consistent as she thought it was.

Rey did this to keep her mind off of everything that was going on, off of the muffled voices behind the door, off of the fear that her father was going to be taken away from her. He sat in the other room, talking with the immigration lawyers.

Since her mother died eight years ago, her father had been the one constant and stable thing in her life. She was about to turn fifteen. They were planning her big *Quinceañera* when a knock came on their apartment door.

Rey's father answered. There was a woman standing in front of him, wearing a pantsuit. He was handed an envelope. He was flabbergasted. Rey kept hearing her father say that he was a citizen, over and over again.

The woman didn't say anything but, "You have to turn yourself in."

Rey's father shook his head and refused. That's why they were at the immigration lawyer's office. Rey's father didn't want to get wrongfully deported.

"Are you really a citizen, *Papí?*" Rey asked her father as they drove home.

"Yes. I came here with proper papers. I even have a permanent resident card. They got the wrong person."

"Are you going to be deported?"

"No, *mija*, I will never leave you. The lawyers will get things sorted. Don't worry."

Rey sat in her seat in silence. She was too worried. She was scared that she would come home from school tomorrow and her father wouldn't be there. A student at her school had that happen to them. They came to school the next day crying and in the same clothes they had on the day before.

Miss Hawthorne, her principal, took in the student and gave them a temporary home until they sort out what happened. The student is still living with her.

Rey didn't want that to happen to her. She knew if her dad were taken away, she'd be put into someone else's home. She had no other family here. Her parents were the first to move out of Mexico.

She was irritated with that woman that came to the door. Her parents did everything by the book. The only thing her father said he hasn't done was become naturalized... he said he was saving up his money to do so, but he wanted to give Rey her *Quinceañera* first.

She felt guilty that all this was happening because of some stupid party.

"We don't have to have a *quince*. We can get you naturalized and then have a party afterwards. Double celebration," Rey suggested. Her father shook his head and smiled at Rey. His eyes watered.

"Rey, please don't worry about this. Everything will be sorted out. I promise."

Rey nodded as she tried to put her mind somewhere else. It was hard not to think about it. Especially since the memory of that student coming in crying kept popping into her mind like a broken record. Rey couldn't shake their words from her head.

"They took them away. I didn't know what to do. There was no food... I had no one to call..."

When they finally got back to their apartment Rey tried working on some homework as her father sat at the table filling out paper work. He was also talking to her grandfather on the phone.

Rey could barely understand what he was saying. She never really spoke Spanish. They used to speak it a lot at home, but after her mother died, her dad only spoke English. Her mom hadn't taken the time to fully learn English; she was too stubborn. But since her dad worked as an engineer, he had to be able to communicate in English with everyone. He learned to speak it fluently within a month.

Rey only remembered a few phrases, but that was it.

Her father sounded exasperated and he slammed his fist against the table a couple times. Rey watched as he ended the call on his cellphone. His shoulders slumped.

"What's wrong, *Papí*?"

"Oh, it's nothing."

"Dad?"

"*Abuelo* wanted some extra cash. I told him about the situation I'm in and that I couldn't afford to send him anything. He just scolded me for being a terrible son."

"Doesn't he understand what's going on?"

"He does. He's just being selfish. I guess I was also enabling him a bit over the years. Your mother was right." He chuckled dryly.

Rey sat at the table with her father.

"She always used to say that I was too much of a pushover with your *abuelo*."

"Are you sure... we're okay?"

"Stop asking me that. I'll start to doubt it myself!"

"I just..." Rey's tears broke through the barrier she was trying to build up. "I just don't want to end up alone."

Rey's father took her in his arms and squeezed her tight. He let her cry into his chest for a few seconds before finally speaking.

"Reina. Believe in this system. There's a reason why things run they way they do. If we cannot trust the system, then there would be complete chaos. This was just a case of mistaken identity, I assure you... I have the best lawyers... and a great boss who is willing to advocate for me. We will not be torn apart. Okay?"

Rey nodded into his chest. She always felt safe in his arms. She trusted everything that he said.

That night, she went to bed with her worries pushed aside.

The next morning, Rey said goodbye to her father as she hopped out of the car to go to school. She took a deep breath as she entered her building. Her previous worries crept into the back of her mind.

"Hey, Rey!" Her best friend, Mallory, greeted as she approached her locker. Mallory's smile and energy was enough to wash away any doubts in Rey. "What's up?"

"Nothing much."

"Did you ask your dad if you could have the party?"

"Yeah, he said that he's been saving for it." Rey smiled.

"No way! See, you were so worried." Mallory's eyes lit up. "I can't wait to help plan it with you. I get to be a part of your dancers right?"

"Of course! It'll probably just be you since you're my only friend." Rey chuckled.

"You should come over after school, we'll start practicing." Mallory danced a little beside Rey as they walked to their first class.

Rey laughed. All the worries she was thinking about before had disappeared... and then suddenly came back when at lunch, her principal came to talk with her.

"Reina, honey, I need you to come with me to the office." Miss Hawthorne had a smile on her face but her eyes told a different story. Rey looked up at Miss Hawthorne and knew exactly what she wanted to talk about.

They took her father.

In the office Miss Hawthorne sat tall in her chair as she read through paperwork sat in front of her.

"So, your dad's lawyers faxed this over to us." She handed the papers over to Rey. Rey looked them over. It was a letter written to her from her father.

It explained that even though they're going through the court process to prove mistaken identity, he had to be detained. He said they had funds to make bail, so to not worry about him being gone for long. Their family friends, the Johnsons will handle it and in the meantime she will stay at their house.

Rey's tears fell down her cheeks as she kept reading. Her dad said how sorry he was that he had to be gone for a bit and that he loved her and would see her soon. He also apologized that they wouldn't be able to do the big *quince* they were planning. Rey shook her head after reading that part. She didn't care. She just wanted her father home.

"Mrs. Johnson is coming to pick you up. We agreed that it'll be hard for you to concentrate with all this on your mind today." Miss Hawthorne reached across the desk and placed a hand on Rey's. "If you need anything during this, don't hesitate to come to me, okay?"

Rey nodded and wiped her tears.

"Can I wait in here?"

"Yes, hon, you can stay right here. I'll send someone to grab your stuff for you."

Miss Hawthorne walked out of the office and left Rey alone with the papers. Some were full of legal terms that Rey didn't understand, but they were important and her father said to hold on to them.

Mrs. Johnson showed up a few moments later. She came into the office and immediately wrapped Rey in her arms. Rey started crying again.

"Sweet girl, everything will be okay. Let's get you home and we'll discuss everything you have questions about."

Rey nodded and followed Mrs. Johnson out to her car. The drive was silent. Rey didn't know what to really say. She had a thousand questions running through her head.

The main question was: Will he be sent to Mexico?

Mrs. Johnson shook her head while she took a sip of her sweet tea. Rey sat curled up in her favorite chair at the Johnson's house.

They had been close with Rey and her father since her mother met Mrs. Johnson at work. Every weekend they would spend Sunday dinner at their house. It helped that Mrs. Johnson spoke Spanish; she was the only person that was close to Rey's mom at the nursing home they worked at.

"Craig and I will do whatever we can to help your dad. He's already got great lawyers. It's just a matter of due process. Craig is over at the bail bonds place right now working out getting your dad home."

"Trust the system, he said."

"Yes, we have to have faith."

"What if... What if they don't believe us?"

"Then we'll give them hell." Mrs. Johnson smirked as Rey eyes widen in shock. Rey chuckled a little.

"Thanks for letting me stay here, Mrs. Johnson."

"Child! How many times do I have to tell you to call me Henrietta?" Mrs. Johnson poured some more sweet tea in her glass from the pitcher that sat in front of them.

"Mamá always said to call you Mrs. Johnson." Rey looked down at her lap. Mrs. Johnson got up from her chair and wrapped Rey in her arms again.

"Call me whatever you like, Reina. I'll still love you."

Rey started to feel tired and made her way into the guest room. She curled up on the bed and quickly dozed off.

* * *

Rey slowly opened her eyes to Mrs. Johnson sitting on the bed beside her, gently nudging her awake. She said they'd go by the apartment later to grab her a set of clothes to change into. She still insisted that Rey wasn't going to stay there too long.

Emi Sano

After walking through her empty apartment she was hit with a crashing tidal wave of the unknown. She didn't know how much clothes to grab or if she should grab some of their invaluable things from the apartment for safekeeping.

She wanted to take all the pictures from the walls. She wanted to have everything from that apartment and move into the tiny guest room at the Johnson's.

In the end she grabbed a few days worth of clothes, her books, and computer.

When they returned to the Johnson's home, Rey booted up her laptop and got bombarded with Mallory's messages. Rey was about to respond, but Mr. Johnson came back from the bail bonds place with bad news: Immigration had already moved her father.

Rey cried herself to sleep that night.

She tried talking with Mallory on the phone before going to bed, but Mallory wasn't able to understand what was going on. Why should she? She was white; her parents were born in the United States. She didn't have to worry about her dad being taken away and sent to his home country.

She cried so hard that she couldn't speak the next morning and her eyes were red and swollen.

Rey walked around the Johnson's home as she waited for Mrs. Johnson to be ready to take her to school. She saw a picture of Rey, her mom and her father in front of the Christmas tree at her mom's work.

Rey remembered that was the day when she told her mom that she wanted to be called Rey instead of Reina. Her mom was dumbfounded.

She was six years old. Santa had just told her that since she was a good pretty girl, she would get a doll for Christmas... Rey wanted a soccer ball.

"No, *mija*, Rey means king! You are queen, Reina."

"But I don't wanna be a queen. Queens are just pretty girls. I wanna be strong like a King!" Rey flexed her arms and roared like a lion. Her mom laughed. It was one of the last memories she had of her mom before she got sick.

Rey lay down on the guest bed staring up at the ceiling. She didn't feel like a king now. She felt weak.

Her father was missing. They moved him to a new facility and his lawyers couldn't get any information to where they sent him. They said immigration was dragging their feet. Rey felt like giving up faith in the system. It didn't feel like they were being treated fairly at all. It felt like they were just road trash being thrown around in the wind.

Mrs. Johnson tiptoed around Rey after they found out they couldn't bring him home. She made Rey's favorite meal, chicken mac and cheese, but didn't say a word during dinner. Rey felt uncomfortable. She wondered if that's how the other student felt at Miss Hawthorne's.

After three long agonizing days, they were able to get in contact with her father. They moved him to another state. They were processing him as if he were going to be deported. Rey felt her heart drop into her stomach.

"Don't worry," he said, his voice staticky through the phone. "I will get to meet with the judge in a couple days. My lawyers will be there. We will show them my records and my legal status; it will be fine. I'll be home soon, I promise."

"Stop making promises," Rey said before handing the phone to Mr. Johnson.

Rey ran to the guest room and shut herself in the rest of the day. She felt terrible about what she had said... if those were to be her last words with him.

She just didn't want to get disappointed.

Rey went to school the next day. Miss Hawthorne asked if everything was all right. All Rey felt she could do was nod and put on her best smile before continuing to her class.

Mallory was furious when she heard what happened. She looked down at her feet before meeting eyes with Rey, "I'm sorry this is happening to you."

"It's okay. My dad said he'd get it sorted out. So I'll just have to wait a bit."

"Well, my father said that if you need our help, he'd be happy to make some calls."

"Thanks, Mallory, but I think we'll be okay."

"Sure."

The air around them became awkward. It was the first time they both had to deal with a problem that neither could relate to. It was the first time they realized they weren't the same.

The courthouse waiting area had a flickering light. Rey sat there and stared at it. She felt as if it were an ominous sign. The annoying flickering light was as sporadic as the one in the lawyer's office.

Mrs. Johnson told her it was time for the hearing and they quickly ushered themselves into the courtroom. Rey and Mrs. Johnson placed themselves in the pew a few rows behind the defense table. Rey noticed there were other people in the room that she didn't recognize. She asked Mrs. Johnson about the people and was told that they were there for other cases. She was about to ask why they weren't waiting outside, when her father was being escorted in.

Rey's father walked out wearing an orange jumpsuit. He was cuffed like a criminal.

Rey's eyes began to water as she saw him look weak and defeated.

Did they hurt him? She wondered.

When Rey's father noticed Rey sitting behind him he started to cry.

The lawyers spoke most of the time. They were up with the judge. She couldn't hear anything they were talking about. Rey and her father just locked eyes while the lawyers were talking.

Rey's father mouthed, "I'm sorry, I love you."

Rey nodded.

"This is fucking ridiculous!" Her father's lawyer said furiously.

"I won't have that kind of language in my court, Mr. Stein." The judge crossed his arms.

Her father's lawyer returned to his argument in a quieter tone.

Rey looked over at Mrs. Johnson. "They don't believe him."

"No, they do. They will. They have to," Mrs. Johnson said, but she was also looking worried. She repeated, "They have to."

The lawyers returned to their prospective places. The judge asked Rey's father to stand up.

"Mr. Javier Gomez, have you ever received a conviction?"

"No, sir. Not even a parking ticket," her father replied humbly.

"Do you believe, whole-heartedly, that you have been falsely identified? Tell the truth in this court."

"Yes, sir. I have been wrongly accused as being undocumented. I have all my records with me. I have been working hard to become a naturalized citizen, sir."

"I believe you," The judge said as gasps escaped out of the Johnsons and Rey. "I'm so sorry that they have put you in this situation. You are free to go home to your family, Mr. Gomez. The state is ordered to grant you your missing two week's worth of pay plus refund of your lawyer's retainer fee. This was an outrageous mistake on their end, but make sure you get your citizenship soon, so I don't have to see your face again."

"Yes, sir." Rey's father turned around and let out a relieved breath. He caught Rey's eye and smiled. She smiled back.

Her heart rate returned to normal. It was a crazy feeling she got, like a large weight came off her shoulders. Rey got up from her seat and ran towards the defense table as her father finished hugging his lawyers.

"I thought things were going south when you made your outburst," he said to Mr. Stein.

"Yeah, I know, I just was starting to get pissed off that the judge seemed like he was agreeing with the prosecutor." His lawyer looked apologetic.

"*Papi!*" Rey exclaimed when she finally made it to her father. They embraced for what seemed like a century. Rey's tears fell effortlessly.

"I told you I'd be home soon," Her father said as he brushed his fingers through Rey's hair. Rey nodded into his chest. "Come on, I have to go back to the prison so I can get processed out and then I'll see you outside the building, okay?"

Rey pulled away from her father. She took one last look at him before he returned to the room he was sitting in prior.

The system worked, Rey thought. It was a relief.

Back in their apartment, Rey sat with her father at the table. They were going through the citizenship test. Rey chuckled when she knew some of the answers before her father.

A knock came to the door. Rey and her father exchanged glances.

"It's just us!" exclaimed Mrs. Johnson.

They both let out the breath they were holding. Rey ran to the door and let them in. It was Sunday night, after all.

FRIENDS

DOROTHY

DOROTHY WAS MY BEST FRIEND. We had met in school when were ten and were forced to sit next to each other when she came in on her first day. It was hard at first to get to know her because I was mad she took my other friend, Charlene's seat.

Dorothy was black and I was white. It was the first time our district was integrating students. We were one of the later schools to do so in our state. My parents were strong supporters of this movement, but we knew a lot of others who were against it. Before the integration, my parents became friends with our black neighbors who moved in during the suburban housing boom. Even though their children were much older than I, my parents still let me play with them.

It was scary when I went to school on the first day of integration. My father walked me in through the crowds of people who were protesting. They were screaming at all the black children and parents who were walking into the school. I held onto my father's hand so tight, I thought it would break. He held me close to him as we entered. I couldn't believe the people I saw at the picket line. Folks I went to church with had the look of malice on their faces, like lions readying for a kill. I never saw them the same way again.

Dorothy and I first talked on the playground; Charlene and I were trying out this new jump rope song and I asked Dorothy if she wanted to join. She was standing by herself against the wall, watching us play. Dorothy was the only black student in my grade; all the others were much older than us. Charlene was nervous about letting Dorothy use her jump rope, but when we saw her nail every hop, skip and spin, it didn't matter.

> *"Cinderella, dressed in yellow*
> *went upstairs to kiss a 'fella*
> *made a mistake*
> *and kissed a snake*
> *how many doctors*
> *did it take?"*

Dorothy made it all the way to twenty before she tripped the rope. She became the jump rope queen.

Charlene's parents didn't want her to associate with Dorothy, so after a while we didn't see much of her. She was later pulled out of the school.

One day, Dorothy and I went to a soda shoppe after school. We decided to split a strawberry milkshake because it was all we could afford with our allowances. So we were sipping on our own straws and giggling over the gurgling noise it made.

A tall man, whom I later found his name was Mr. Mitchell, came in to the shoppe and grabbed onto both of our arms to pull us away from each other. He was yelling at Dorothy for sharing a drink with me.

"What in God's name is goin' on in this shoppe? I can't have this goin' on in my town. Y'all shouldn't be sharin' anythin', y'hear?" He was fuming. We were both really scared.

I yanked my arm out of his hand and stood in front of Dorothy as she cowered, which was something I've never seen her do before. Dorothy was never scared of anything. Later, I had found out her mama told her to never talk back to the white men, so she was pretending to be scared to protect herself.

I told Mr. Mitchell that she was my best friend and we could share what we wanted. He took a hold of my shoulders and shook my body saying I needed to be disciplined. He was about to slap me when the shoppe owner, Mr. Larson, came from out back with a rifle and told Mr. Mitchell to please leave.

When Mr. Mitchell left, Mr. Larson apologized to us and said our shake was free. He urged us to run on home and don't stop or look back until we got there.

I grabbed Dorothy's hand and we ran. We didn't stop running until we got to her house, which was closer than mine. We made sure the door was locked before we hugged and finally allowed ourselves to cry.

Dorothy's mama came in the hall from the kitchen and saw the tears streaking our faces. She asked what had happened. Dorothy explained it all. I kept apologizing through my sobs, terrified she wouldn't let us be friends. Dorothy's mama looked up at me. She opened her arms out for me to go in and she hugged us both tightly. She told us that there would always be people in the world who don't want us to be friends. As long as we stayed together we would always win.

It was the first time I met Dorothy's mama. She reminded me a lot like my mama: smart, strong, and beautiful. I gave Dorothy's papa a fright when he came home from work. He wasn't expecting me to be in their home but he wasn't as scary as Dorothy said he'd be. Dorothy's papa laughed when we told him the story about Mr. Mitchell at Mr. Larson's soda shoppe. He asked Dorothy why she didn't say something, and Dorothy's mama shot out from the kitchen, "Because I told her to keep her big mouth shut in public." That sent Dorothy's papa howling in laughter again.

My parents loved that I had found an honest to God good friend. We were free to go back and forth to each other's homes. My mama would always have a fresh batch of Dorothy's favorite, snickerdoodle cookies, waiting for whenever she'd come over. And Dorothy's mama would make sure we had our fill of sweet iced tea and lemon bars during the hazy summers.

Eventually both our parents started meeting with each other and they all became friends. Most folks in the town weren't too bothered by our presence together, but there were some who would openly voice their frustrations to my father.

My father was a prideful man. He always carried himself with dignity and whenever someone tried to knock him down, he wouldn't let it affect him.

One day, Mr. Mitchell stormed up to my father and cussed him out for letting me be

Dorothy's friend. My father didn't say anything but, "Is that all?" back to Mr. Mitchell. When Mr. Mitchell left, my father took this as an opportunity to teach us a lesson.

He said, "Now, what that man said there was hurtful. I'm not denying that. But if someone makes you happy, you shouldn't be embarrassed or try to hide that friendship. Don't let others tell you who to love."

We both nodded and smiled at each other.

"One day, people won't care who you're friends with. That day will come for you two, don't you worry." My father patted the top of our heads and walked on down the street.

Dorothy and I told her mama about it the next day and she agreed. She said that she prayed for it every day.

While the civil rights movement gained traction, we would listen to the news about Dr. Martin Luther King Jr. leading marches and encouraging peaceful protests. He was preaching that we should all live together peacefully and equally. Dorothy and I imagined being a part of the marches. Our mamas would never let us participate, but we still pretended.

Dorothy was outspoken during class debates on the civil rights movement. I stepped in whenever I felt like she was being outnumbered. It got us into a lot of trouble, but Dorothy never backed down from an argument. I was honored to be able to stand by my friend's side.

When Dr. Martin Luther King Jr. was assassinated, we both sobbed. It was like someone had killed the idea of our friendship. Dorothy's mama wouldn't let us outside for the entire day. She was afraid something bad was going to happen. I stayed the night at her house. The next day, my father had come to pick me up and escorted me home. Everyone was on edge for the next few weeks, but soon things returned to normal.

After we graduated from high school, we both set out on our different ways... Dorothy went to Howard University and I, well I started at Princeton, but ended up falling in love with a boy, we got married, and I quit school when I got pregnant with my son.

We lost touch along the way, but I always thought about her, if she succeeded in her dreams, and wondered if she did the same with me.

I bumped into Dorothy years later. My husband and I had just moved to another town and had to change doctors. Dorothy was a pediatrician, and we met up again when she became both my son and daughter's doctor. We both laughed over how small the world was that it would bring us back together after so many years.

I learned her papa died a couple years after she got married and her mama was very ill. Both her two daughters were around my children's age. I was surprised she was still able to finish school and work after having children. But I knew that not even being a mother could stop her from helping other folks.

We kept in touch. Our husbands and kids became friends and we celebrated every birthday and holiday as one big family. It was just like how we left off, but no one bothered us for being friends anymore.

As we got older, it was harder for us to see each other. Our kids tried to make sure we met up as often as they could, but for two old folks like us it was nearly impossible to coordinate schedules with our children.

One day, Dorothy's oldest daughter, called me saying her mama was very sick. I immediately had my son drive me out to see her. Dorothy smiled as I held onto her wrinkly hand. I watched this strong woman turn fragile in front of me. It was very hard to see her like that, but I could only imagine how I looked to her. We were old, wrinkly and grey; practically twins.

She told me how happy she was that we had gotten back together after all these years. We reminisced on our younger days when we got into mischief, giving our mamas heart attacks. We laughed together like we used to back in the day.

"You know, if it weren't for you, I don't think I'd be who I am. My mama was so worried sending me to that school, but she knew it was the best chance for me to get a better education. After we played jump rope at recess, I came home to tell my mama I made a friend with a white girl – you – and my mama nearly cried. She still worried every day, but I knew what you and I had was strong."

Dorothy coughed, trying to catch her breath. I told her to save it and we can talk later.

Unfortunately, we never had later.

ISABELA

IT WAS AN ORDINARY DAY FOR YOUNG ISABELA, BUT IT WAS ABOUT TO BECOME EXTRAORDINARY. Isabela went running out into her backyard like she always did after school. She was going to play on her swing set, but a glimmering light caught her eye in the forest.

She decided to run towards that light. To her surprise the light flew off further into the trees. She continued to follow the light until it stopped at a dead tree with a huge hole at the bottom. She watched as the light flew in and disappeared.

Standing beside her was a doe. The doe looked at Isabela for a second before walking into the tree and disappeared.

Curious, Isabela inspected the tree before taking a step into the trunk and out onto a grassy field. To her delight, she was standing on the edge of a forest animal gathering.

An owl stood at the center, shouting for silence as the rest of the animals talked amongst them.

"Silence!! Is everyone here? Whooo are we missing?" The owl continued trying to maintain order.

Isabela saw the doe that walked in before her, went up to her and asked, "Excuse me, can you tell me what's going on?"

The doe looked at her and replied, "We're having a committee meeting to decide who gets to stay in the forest and who has to find a new place to live."

"Why?"

"Because there isn't enough room for all of us and the food have gotten scarce. Surely you've noticed, tiny human."

"My name is Isabela, and no I haven't noticed."

"Well, listen on then." The doe turned her attention back to the center where the owl started its proceedings.

"Hear, hear, I call this meeting to begin. First order of business, whooo has been digging into the Marcos' trash? We all know they're off limits because they just lost their cat, Hector."

The crowd whispered amongst themselves.

"I'm terribly sorry." A small raccoon spoke. "We just couldn't get food last week, my little one was sick. We were afraid it was rabies!" The crowd gasped at the mention of rabies. They stepped back from the raccoon in fear.

"It's all right, Raccoon. We will help you forage for better food." The raccoon responded with a meek thank you and the owl moved on to the next order of business.

"All right, now we're going to talk about why we're all here. As you know, the forest lost another portion last month due to the new housing development. We are currently over populated in certain areas and there have been a few skirmishes in consequence." The owl stopped and looked at the fox and the rabbit families staring off at each other. "We all know we're supposed to cohabit this forest together."

Some animals agreed with stamping feet or grunting.

"Unfortunately, since we are running out of real estate here, we have to vote on who has to move."

All at once the animals started shouting out who they felt should leave.

"Foxes!"

"Owls!"

"Deer!"

"Get rid of the rabbits!"

The owl flapped its wings violently and they all stopped speaking. A rabbit came running up into the center and stood on its hind legs.

"We need to have reasons, we can't just get rid of a species because we don't like them!" More stamping of the feet in agreement followed.

"Very well, the ground is open; why don't you start?" the owl said to the rabbit.

"Certainly." The rabbit started cleaning its ears nervously. "I think we should vote the foxes out."

"THAT'S SPECIST! YOU JUST WANT US OUT BECAUSE WE EAT YOU," a fox shouted back.

The rabbit grew even more nervous, grabbing onto one of its ears as it spoke. "No! That's not it! You guys have taken over too much of our living area. We let you in because they tore down your home, but now you're eating our berries and leaving us with nothing! It's almost snow season, and we need the food to survive!"

"Yeah, and you ate my dear grandmamma last winter!" A field mouse squeaked as loud as it could. "Couldn't you have waited one more winter? She was only 2 years old!"

"I'll eat you next!" The fox snarled back. The field mouse squeaked in fear and ran to hide behind a moose.

"Order! Order!" The owl shrieked. "Who else has something to say?"

"Excuse me?" Isabela said as she started to walk towards the center of the field. Some animals flinched in fear as she walked by. "Where are these animals going once you've voted them out?"

The owl puffed out its chest. "They find another forest."

"But what if there isn't another. Are you really sure they're surviving?"

The other animals talked amongst themselves in hushed tones.

"This is the only way to preserve forest life, tiny human. You would not understand."

"I understand... enough. But if you're really trying to preserve life, why send them out to the unknown? I remember last year we saw some bears in my backyard! But I'm looking around, and I don't see them here. Why?"

"They left to go into the mountains and away from civilization after their grandfather was shot by a hunter," the doe said as she approached the center. "Your kind has slowly been killing us, whether you realize it or not. We're just trying to survive. My family has either been killed off by hunters or those moving boxes you sit in."

Isabela started to tear up, "How do I make it stop? How can I help?"

"Listen, kid, from the looks of it you're still a child. No one will listen to you. But when you're older, remember us. Remember what we had to do. And then do something," the fox said frankly.

"But that's years from now."

The animals grew silent.

"We'll survive. You just remember what you saw and heard today," the owl said. "I think it's fair we put off the exile this year. Foxes, you can move closer to where the moose live so we can put an end to your skirmish with the rabbits."

The fox and rabbit both nodded and ran off in different directions.

"We'll reconvene after the cold season." The animals all turned around and walked away.

Isabela was left in the center of the field with the owl.

"What if I forget?"

The owl handed her a branch with the golden light surrounding it.

"When you're older, and we meet again, you will see this light up."

Isabela took the branch. The doe motioned her to follow and she went through another tree and out into the forest she was in before. The doe nodded and ran away.

Isabela stood for a few seconds in awe.

"ISABELA? DÓNDE ESTÁS? LA CENA ESTÁ LISTA!" Isabela's mom called out. Isabela stuck the branch into her pocket and she ran back to the house.

"Estoy aquí, mamá!" Isabela called back as she reached the edge of her backyard. Isabela's mom looked relieved as she saw her daughter skip happily into the home.

"Don't you go running off like that again!"

"Sí, mamá."

"Now, go wash up and get the plates for dinner. Papi will be home soon." Isabela nodded and ran up the stairs to wash her hands. She took the branch out of her pocket and set it on her dresser before running into the bathroom.

7 YEARS LATER...

Emi Sano

Isabela, lie on her bed chatting on messenger with one of her friends. A stuffed owl watched her as she texted.

Her teenage room was filled with forest animal photos, both taken by her and from National Geographic magazines. One of the pictures on her wall was of her ten years old self holding a "SAVE THE ANIMALS" sign near a construction site.

Out of the corner of her eye she noticed a light glowing from the top of her dresser. She curiously looked at it and then suddenly remembered.

"IT'S TIME!" Isabela called out to no one in particular. She grabbed the branch and took off running outside.

The branch glowed brighter the further she walked into the forest. The forest looked a lot smaller than she remembered. She took a path that she seemed familiar and the branch lit up.

She stopped right in front of a dead tree. Again, it looked a lot smaller than she remembered.

When she stepped in, she was worried the magic wasn't going to work this time, but she quickly shook that thought out of her head as she stepped through into the open field for the first time in seven years.

There weren't a lot of forest animals around this time: only the deer, rabbits, owl and field mice.

The owl was older looking. Isabela walked in closer to hear what they were discussing.

"Hear, hear! Is everyone here?" The owl stopped when he saw Isabela. "My, how tall you've grown, tiny human."

"What happened?"

"You must be Isabela, my mom told me about you." The buck spoke as he moved closer to Isabela.

"Yes, how is she?"

"She was hit by the moving box..." The buck snorted. "Your people did that."

Isabela shook her head. "Couldn't you have not cross the road? Why would you put the blame on us?"

"YOUR ROAD is going through OUR HOME." That angry voice sounded familiar to Isabela. She turned and saw the same fox hobble towards the group.

"Fox, how nice of you to join us." Owl spoke as if he didn't hear him. "Shall we begin?"

"I'm sorry, but there's not a lot of you, why are you still holding these meetings?" Isabela interrupted.

The owl continued, ignoring Isabela. "We are here today because fox overheard that our beloved forest is about to be bulldozed for more housing. We must all find a new home soon."

Isabela listened and racked her brain for the truth in what the owl was saying and then she remembered seeing a sign showcasing smart homes for the future family.

She silently whispered, "Oh, no! They're doing it again!"

"I scouted another forest just beyond the busy road. If we can all find a way to make it across, we'll be able to live there for a while. The others have found homes in this forest and recommended it." Owl continued on talking about travel arrangements and who would help whom. He promised that he wouldn't eat the field mice as he helps them over to the new forest. The rest all believed they could make it on their own.

"What if I can make it so they don't build here?" Isabela asked. "I've done it once before. I can do it again." She grabbed her phone from her pocket and started snapping photos of the animals. Something she wished she had the first time she wrote a letter to the wildlife conservationists. "I'll take these pictures of you guys and then show them to the developers and I can stop them."

Last time the conservation group listened to Isabela because she was a young girl and they wanted to be a good role model. The developers didn't want bad press so they put a stop to the housing plan.

Isabela was frantic; she couldn't believe they were going to try this again after she did everything to stop them before.

"I'm sorry, but we can't take our chances. We must evacuate before they start knocking down the trees."

"Just give me a week! I can do it!" Isabela took off running back to the tree and without hesitation, ran into it with full speed. She ran out of the dead tree and continued running until she came home.

She went up the stairs past her mom and hopped on to the computer, starting to email all the activists she had contacted when she was little with the help of her mom. Now, at seventeen, she was hoping they remembered her.

The next day she walked over to where the housing development would begin. She stared at all the equipment sitting idle, waiting and ready to work.

They still built houses in the area, even after her protest got the corporations to listen, but they only made half the houses, citing that protecting the ecosystem will be a part of their building plans from then on.

The sign had the same corporation that made the previous homes. A truck had pulled up to the development entrance. The foreman to the construction site walked over to her.

"Can I help you miss?" The foreman asked, "Wait, don't I know you?"

"Are you working here?"

"Yes, I'm in charge."

"I can't let you tear down the last of this forest."

"I do know you, you were the girl that stopped construction several years ago... I'm sorry, but my boss says the land is costing him money. He needs to make money now."

The foreman shook his head and folded his arms. He's dealt with so many of her type these past few years. He was just about to call the police when she put her hand on his arm.

"Please, I urge you to have him reconsider. Build a small park here, or maybe a trail where people can pay to hike! Just don't tear down this forest... it means so much to me."

Isabela took out her phone and showed him pictures of the animals she met with last night. "Look at these animals, they're all in danger of losing their home if you build here!"

She looked into the foreman's eyes. His dark eyes almost mirrored hers. "Please?"

The foreman pulled his arm away from her. He sighed and continued to call.

"Don't call the police! I'm leaving." Isabela walked away, the foreman sighed as he looked back out into the forest. He dialed another number.

Isabela walked into her home, feeling helpless. She had done this so long ago and it only worked because she was ten and the community rallied behind her. Now nobody cared about forest animals. They just wanted more homes to buy.

A PING on her phone notified her of an email. It was a response back from the local nature activist group. They were going to look into the area and see if they could find any loopholes to prevent them from building there. Isabela replied thanks and that she hoped that this would finally put an end to the extinction of these animals.

She looked at the branch the owl gave her so many years ago.

"You will get to keep your home," she said. "I promise."

"Isabela? What are you up to, now?"

"Mom, they're going to build in that forest again! We can't let them do this. The animals have nowhere else to go! They're all going to die."

"Oh sweetie, they were going to build there anyway. They just stopped construction all those years ago was because they didn't want bad publicity."

"Mom!"

"There's nothing you can do. They're going to build regardless. Your uncle just called me; his friend is the foreman and told him what you were doing out there. Do not go back over there or you could get hurt."

Isabela's mouth dropped. "Mom, this is my purpose!"

"Isabela, you are seventeen years old. Your only purpose is to graduate high school and get into a good college!"

"Why can't I have both?" Isabela felt the tears form in her eyes. She didn't want to cry. She didn't want to look weak while trying to fight for something she believed so strongly about.

"You need to stop living in that fairytale world where you talked to animals and they asked for your help. I thought you would outgrow this, Isabela. Just let it go."

"They're dying, mom! All of them!"

"There is nothing you can do. Isabela, please. Just drop it. I won't tell Papi about this." Isabela's mom walked off.

Isabela wanted to scream. This kind of thing was what she wanted to do in life. She wanted to go to school to protect nature and its wildlife. She didn't understand why her mom wouldn't understand.

She got another email from the activist saying they were putting together a protest in a couple of days, and were writing up a proposal for changes to the plan, asking them to reconsider the housing development and make a nature park instead. Isabela smiled and replied that she would be there to help. She hoped she would, anyway.

When her Papi came home from work, Isabela waited until after they had dinner to talk to him about it. If she could convince her papi to understand, she could change the world.

"Papi, do you have a minute?" Isabela asked quietly while he sat reading his book. Her papi looked up from the book and nodded before putting it down.

"What's on your mind, mija?"

"Papi, you know how passionate I am about the wildlife. I'm so passionate. I know this is what I want to do as an adult."

"You want to go to school for what?"

"I want to study wildlife management. I want to work with wildlife conservationists. Is that okay?"

Isabela's papi leaned forward in his chair, feeling the same excitement and passion Isabela was exhibiting. "Of course! This is why we came to America, so you can be who you want to be."

"Great! Now, you know all this, I have something important going on right now, Papi."

"Oh... Isabela..." Her papi sat back in his chair. "Is this about the housing development down the road?"

Isabela's shoulders dropped, she already knew what was going to be said.

"Mija, we have a ton of friends that are working on this project. If you force them to cancel, they all lose their jobs."

"There are other things they can build there that both preserve the wildlife's ecosystem and give the community something.

Like a nature park or – " Isabela was frantic to have someone on her side.

"I understand where you are coming from. Believe me, I do. But you have to think about the people who will be affected as well. I won't stop you from trying. But remember that there are families that are relying on this job." With that being said, Isabela's papi picked up the book and continued reading.

"Thank you, Papi." Isabela got up from the couch and gave him a kiss on the cheek before running out the door.

She ran out into the forest. It was starting to get dark, but she wasn't afraid of getting lost; she knew exactly how far she needed to go..

"Owl! Owl! Are you here?"

Isabella looked around her; maybe they can only meet her in that field. She tried to find the dead tree, but it wasn't where she thought it would be.

"Owl?"

The old owl fluttered in and lands on a low branch near Isabela's head.

"Hoo, hoo," said the owl. Isabela jumped and smiled when she recognized him.

"Owl, I have set up a protest to stop the development. I just need your help."

"Hoo."

"Please, bring everyone to that part of the woods. Let them see you. Let them know who's home they're destroying if they build the houses there. Claim back your land!"

The owl looked away and shook its feathers as to say, "That won't work."

"Don't... give up. Okay? Just bring everyone. The buck, the fox, the rabbits... let the construction workers see you all," Isabela pleaded with the owl. The owl looked back at her and widened its eyes.

"Hoo," he said before stretching his wings and flying back into the forest.

The day of the protest, Isabela was the first to arrive. When the activists came they all greeted each other with the same enthusiasm as they did the first time they showed up.

"Isabela, you've grown so much," said Jessica, the founder of the group. "I'm so glad you gave us another email."

"I didn't know what else to do." Isabela smiled. "Thanks for listening to me again."

"Any time! We all must do what we can to give the wildlife a voice, isn't that right?" Jessica boasted as Isabela nodded.

They walked over to the rest of the group, each member varied in ages, only a couple of them were close to Isabela in age.

"Hey, you're going to join the group after high school?" one boy asked.

"I'm going to college first, get more knowledge, then I'll see from there."

"Well, we could use you," he said as he walked off to go pass out signs for the others to hold.

The protest began and at first, none of the construction workers were there, but then soon enough the foreman arrived, looking annoyed as ever.

"We have a permit to protest here." Jessica held up a piece of paper signed by the town clerk. "So you can't call the police on us."

The foreman shook his head and saw Isabela. "I'm going to call your parents."

"Do it! They already know I'm here."

Soon, press came to cover what was happening in this small neighborhood. Some remembered what conspired here years prior and were making it a big story. A ton of people from the neighborhood came to watch as the protesters shouted phrases like, "Don't destroy homes to build your home!" and "Be kind to every kind, not just mankind!"

Isabela added to the shouts with a smile on her face. She couldn't believe the amount of supporters that joined them who weren't a part of the protest in the beginning. Her friends showed up and joined the protest. It was exhilarating.

Then a hush came over the crowd when one of the bulldozers started up. Jessica grabbed onto Isabela, shielding her from any harm that might come as the bulldozer started towards the protest.

The group started shouting over the noise and walking towards the bulldozer, but before they could meet up a herd of deer ran into the middle of them. The bulldozer stopped abruptly. Everyone was quiet. Within the herd, there were raccoons and foxes all standing together in between the bulldozer and the forest. They all stood on their four legs, strong and unwilling to move.

Isabela couldn't believe her eyes. The owl had done it. He convinced the animals to show. More animals arrived; it almost looked like the first time she went to their annual eviction meeting. Squirrels, more owls, wildcats, bears, birds, every forest animal you can imagine all standing in solidarity. None of them were thinking of hunting each other, they all stood to protect their home.

The driver of the bulldozer stepped out and knelt to the ground in shock.

Shortly after, more people joined the protest with the animals. "Don't destroy homes to build your homes!"

The president of the company that bought this land stepped in front of the crowd. He had seen what the animals have done, and wanted to let everyone know he would not build the housing development. He made a press release that he would instead turn this into a nature preserve and will create a park for humans and wildlife to enjoy.

Cheers erupted after the announcement. Isabela cried tears of joy. She looked over to the forest and saw the animals start to retreat. She found the old owl that ruffled his feathers and it looked like he nodded at her.

"You're welcome," she whispered as he too, retreated back into the forest.

Isabela's parents were pushing through the crowd with tears in their eyes and hearts filled with pride.

"I'm so sorry about what I said, Isabela," her mom said through tears. "You are the change. Be the change."

"I'm proud of you, mija." Isabela's Papi gave her a big hug. "You did great out there, and showed me that you will succeed in your dreams."

Isabela smiled as she watched the bulldozer drive away from the forest. The president of the company walked over to Isabela and her parents with Jessica in tow.

"Miss Isabela, is that right?" he asked as he reached out to shake hands. Isabela shook his hand.

"Yes, sir," she replied courteously.

"Congratulations on changing mine and the board's minds about what to do with this plot of land. If you are looking for a job after you graduate, give us a call. We could definitely use a wildlife conservationist in our team to prevent future mix-ups like this."

Isabela beamed. "I appreciate the offer!"

The president handed her his business card and walked away.

"You did it, Isabela! You've changed someone's mind!" Jessica exclaimed. "I'm so proud of your dedication. You guys must be so proud of your daughter."

Her parents gleamed with pride. "Of course, we'll never doubt her abilities again."

At the end of the day, Isabela and her parents sat quietly in the house, still reeling from the events that took place earlier.

Isabela heard a noise, it sounded like a faint "hoo, hoo". She perked up and went to the backyard.

"Isabela? What is it?" her mom asked and followed her.

In the backyard a few forest animals stood in view. The buck, the fox, and the rabbit all placed a "gift" in the middle of them. They were branches and berries.

Isabela walked out towards them, much to her mom's dismay, with a smile on her face she reached out and touched each one's head gently. They all showed their own form of endearment gesture.

"Welcome home."

THE END.

PETER

SUCK IT UP. Be a man. You're lucky she even looked at you. Just shrug it off and move to the next person. Peter thought to himself as he carried his beer with him away from the bar. He felt humiliated. All he wanted to do was to start a conversation with the girl waiting for a drink next to him. It was something he was trying to work on. His social anxiety made it hard for him to even talk to anyone... let alone women.

He took a huge gulp of liquid courage and continued through the crowd. His therapist suggested that he should do this at least once a week to get more acclimated in social situations. She gave him a list of topics to talk about with strangers.

The first topic he tried?

"What happened with the Orioles last night... am I right?"

"What?" She gave Peter a weirded out look, "They won last night against the Rays."

"Oh... yeah, I know that's what I mean! They've been doing pretty shitty lately... am I right?"

"Yeah..." the woman walked away without ordering a drink.

Peter kicked himself about that conversation. He knew talking about sports was a bad idea. He wasn't really into sports... having social anxiety and all... it wasn't a good idea for him to attend sport games on the regular.

He scanned his eyes for his next experiment. He liked to call them experiments because he wasn't really into doing this for pleasure. It was more of an assignment for a sociology class.

A group of men his age were hanging out around the pool table and he felt that they seemed okay enough to approach. One was smoking a cigar and talking with a funny northern accent.

"Ah! You shanked it, sir! My turn." The cigar man spoke as he grabbed the cue ball from one of the pockets and placed it on the table. Except, he was placing the ball on the wrong side and Peter knew this.

Peter knew all the rules to play billiards because it was the only thing he played on his computer.

"You're supposed to put the ball on the other side of the table. That wasn't a free for all foul." Peter chirped softly. The cigar guy stopped before hitting the cue ball and looked at Peter.

Peter wasn't a really tiny guy. He was average high, medium build, with a little weight on him. He regularly exercised at home in his free time, so on the outside he didn't seem like someone you can easily push over. The cigar guy seemed to like Peter's presence and moved the cue ball to the correct side of the table.

"Hey thanks for that, man. We didn't know how the rules worked." The cigar guy said as he was setting up for the hit. "Want to play winner and you can show us how to really play?"

Peter wanted to vomit. This group of guys was actually accepting him and he didn't use any of the talking points his therapist gave him.

"Sure," Peter mustered out. He was terrified but he kept telling himself that he needed to do this to get better.

The rest of the group introduced themselves; the cigar guy was actually named Mitch. Then there was Bobby, Hank, and Sean. They were all drinking beers and playing darts and billiards.

Peter didn't know what to do while he waited for his turn. He stood awkwardly as Mitch and Hank played out their game.

"Is it true that if you hit someone else's ball without hitting yours you forfeit the turn?" Hank asked as he sank his striped ball in.

"Yup." Peter said curtly.

"See! I told you!" Hank pointed his stick at Bobby he was aiming up for a throw. Bobby threw his dart that missed the target completely and turned to Hank.

"Hey man! I thought all balls were fair game!"

"You suck at pool, just like you suck at darts."

Peter let out a nervous chuckle. Was this what it felt like to have friends?

Peter felt that sensation of vomiting again and he knew that he had to leave. It was terrible timing because he was just about to start playing against Mitch.

"I'm sorry, guys, I uh... didn't realize the time. I have to get going."

"Ah! You got a girl at home waiting?" Sean asked as Peter tried to walk away.

"No, I have an early day tomorrow. See you around. Thanks for letting me watch." Peter said quickly and took off before anyone could say anything else.

He did it. He could tell his therapist that he had a successful night. He was hoping she would stop assigning those tasks, but he knew it wasn't going to be like that. Peter was in therapy for his social anxiety and to help him overcome that anxiety... he needed to be social.

As he lay on the bed, Peter wondered if he'd see those guys again. They seemed pretty cool. They were at least nice enough to let him join their fun. He felt a little ashamed that he had to bail before he could play with them.

His therapist was a little annoyed he didn't get their contact information to possibly connect again in the future. Peter hadn't even thought of that.

After the session he sat at home, beating himself up mentally over the fact that he didn't get those guys' numbers. He asked his therapist if that was an okay thing to do, since he wasn't asking to go on a date with them or anything. His therapist smiled a little, trying to stifle a chuckle before telling him that it's perfectly normal to ask for someone's number.

Peter couldn't tell if she was going to laugh at him or just at the situation. He hated not understanding social cues. That made him feel very upset, but he didn't mention that to his therapist. He didn't want to upset her as well. After all, she was doing her best to help him.

His homework assignment was to attend a social setting and exchange contact information with at least two people. His therapist told Peter that if he didn't have to use the conversation starters they came up with if he didn't feel comfortable. She told him to be himself – as much of himself as he can to be social.

So, the next weekend, Peter set out to check off the boxes on his to do list. He returned to the same bar as he went the week before. He secretly hoped he would run into those guys again so that his contact information exchange would be easier for him.

Unfortunately, he didn't see Mitch, Bobby, Hank or Sean. Peter walked around awkwardly by the pool table, waiting for those guys to show up. After two hours of standing around, Peter told himself to get out and start mingling. He needed to get two different people's contact information or his therapist would think he wasn't trying.

The thought of talking to total strangers again was terrifying. Peter's heart started racing as he looked around for someone to approach. He wondered what he looked like on the outside. Did he look as freaked out as he felt on the inside?

Somehow, Peter made his way to the bar counter and sat. He really didn't want to go through with this assignment. It was embarrassing enough to have to stammer through introductions.

The bartender walked over to Peter. She smiled at him gently as she placed another beer in front of him.

"Oh, I didn't order one."

"It's okay, it's on me. You look like you could use some more courage."

"I do? Damn. I was hoping it was just happening on the inside." Peter looked down at his hands.

The bartender laughed. "I've seen you here a few times, now. What's up?"

"I'm supposed to get over my social anxiety by... being social with people. My therapist wants me to exchange contact information with a couple people tonight." Peter spit out the truth. He caught himself at the end but it was too late. She already knew.

"Wow! What a task, huh? I have social anxiety, too. It sucks."

"You?"

"What? Cuz I work as a bartender, I can't have social anxiety? Psh." She rolled her eyes. "I'm on like four kinds of medication just so I can function at work. It helps when I can drink while on the job... My name's Ali. You?"

"P-Peter." Peter stuttered out.

"Well, Peter... can I be your first contact exchange?"

Peter was astounded. How did this happen? Why was Ali being so nice? And was she serious about having social anxiety? It took a few moments before Peter could register what was happening before he took out his phone and handed it over to Ali.

Ali typed in her contact information and handed the phone back to Peter. He stared at her name and number, still in shock. This was the first time a woman had ever given him a phone number.

"Thanks." Peter mustered out finally.

Ali nodded, "Now don't forget to send me a text so I can have yours."

She walked off to tend to the rest of the bar as he quickly sent her a text.

Peter couldn't help but smile. This was the first time he didn't feel like puking, too. He wondered if this going out thing every weekend was really working.

"Hey isn't that the pool boy?" Peter heard someone ask behind him. He turned around and recognized Sean standing with Mitch.

Mitch and Peter locked eyes and Mitch nodded his head in acknowledgement. Mitch and Sean started their approach to Peter.

Still riding from the high of getting Ali's number, Peter didn't feel as nervous as he was when he first met these guys. Mitch stuck out his hand for a shake and Peter hesitantly grabbed it.

"Hey man, how's it going? I forgot your name, I'm sorry," Mitch said as he leaned against the bar.

"It's Peter."

"Peter! Dude you bailed on us right before you got to play! We were hoping to see your sick skills in action," Sean chimed in right before ordering his beer from Ali.

Peter smiled nervously and nodded. His nerves were starting to come back but he swallowed them down.

"Yeah, sorry. I think I had a bad drink or something. I didn't feel well," Peter lied as he locked eyes with Ali when she handed the guys their beers. Ali looked concerned and mouthed, "Are you okay?"

Peter nodded to her and she smiled before walking off.

"Well, are you in for a game tonight?" Mitch asked with a smirk.

"Yeah, sure." Peter tried to smile again. He followed the guys towards the back of the bar where the pool tables were.

He wasn't sure why he was so nervous about being around these guys. They were nice. They didn't seem like they were out to make his life miserable. It was weird to him, still, that these guys would be so nice to a stranger. Back in his high school and college days, if he'd ran into guys like them, he'd get put in the trash can.

Mitch had Peter break the balls to start the game. Peter wasn't nervous about playing. He was more nervous about the small talk that came with the playing. The best part about playing billiards online was the lack of small talk.

Peter mainly kept the talking about how to play. The guys were really eager to learn. They told him that they haven't really been playing the real game because no one had bothered to teach them. They were just playing to hit the balls in the pockets as hard as they can.

Peter laughed and told them it isn't about hitting the ball hard, it's about hitting the cue ball at just the right angle and speed to get it to go where you want.

"So, it involves a lot of physics, huh?" Mitch asked as he lined up his next shot.

"Yeah, and geometry. Pretty much all the math stuff we thought we didn't have to use in real life." Peter chuckled.

"Okay, I get it." Mitch eyed the cue ball and his target. He took his time and then hit his target dead on, landing his ball into the side pocket. "WHAT?! I can't believe that worked!"

"Nice one," Peter complimented Mitch on his shot.

"Yeah, after you mentioned the physics and geometry it made sense. I'm a freaking engineer and I didn't get it right away. What do you do?"

Peter's heart started racing. *It's a normal question*, Peter thought, *just answer it*.

"I work in coding. I get to work from home mostly."

"Sweet! I'm in coding, too!" Sean chimed in. "I knew you were a cool dude. Hey want to come with us to this other bar? They have really good food and I'm starving."

Peter struggled against his instinct to chicken out. "Sure, why not?"

"So, what company snagged you?" Sean asked as they were walking out the bar.

Peter did his best to explain that he was a contractor, but didn't want to tell them it was because he didn't want to go to an actual office. Sean was extremely jealous at the idea of being able to work for multiple companies and from home.

"I bet you see a lot of different styles of code."

"Yeah, some of the coders are idiots though. I have to fix a lot before I can do my job."

"Don't I know it," Sean laughed.

Peter got a text on his phone from Ali.

ALI: Saw you leaving with new friends?

PETER: I'm terrified.

ALI: You'll do great. ☺

Peter put his phone back in his pocket and continued his conversation with Mitch and Sean as they made their way to the next pub. His hands were a little shaky as he walked along beside them. Sean and Mitch didn't seem to notice how nervous Peter was, or if they did, they didn't seem to care.

"So, where did you guys go to school?" Peter decided to ask as they rounded the corner to next block.

"Rensselaer Polytechnic Institute. We both went there, that's how we met. Just a couple nerds."

"Don't take it the wrong way, but you guys don't seem like the RPI kind of guys…"

"Dude. We got that all the time. But it's all good. Is that why you bailed on us last weekend?" Mitch asked playfully.

Peter shrugged his shoulders.

"Don't laugh," Peter started off, "but I have social anxiety and you guys were the first people that actually made me not want to vomit… at first."

"See, Bobby and Hank, they're meeting us at the next bar; they thought we scared you off." Sean looked over at Peter.

"Well you guys didn't really scare me off. I'm still trying to work it out. Sorry if I offended you guys by leaving."

"Nah, we get it. We're nerds, remember? It was tough for us in high school, too." Sean smiled.

"Yeah, just because I look like a jock doesn't mean I was one in high school. It took years in college and after graduation to get to where I'm at today." Mitch laughed as he flexed his arms.

Peter's hands stopped shaking. He felt comfortable as time continued. He found the right type of people to be around. Peter felt lucky that he met Mitch and his friends that night, otherwise he didn't know what he'd be doing if he hadn't.

Probably playing a game of billiards online.

LANA

ONE DAY WE WERE THE BEST OF FRIENDS AND THE NEXT, WE HARDLY KNEW EACH OTHER.

I wasn't sure what to do when I saw her at school. Was it okay if I said, "hi," or were we not supposed to speak at all? It was tough walking into a building that seemed small when you had friends around you, but now looked huge and overwhelming when you were alone.

Waiting for homeroom to start was torture. Everyone was hanging around in the halls with their group of friends, waiting for the bell to ring and making plans for later. Except, I was just left wandering the halls, looking for a group to fit in. My slightly worn Converse slapped the floor with a quiet pitter-patter as I subtly eavesdropped on conversations that I could easily slide into.

Unfortunately, after my second rotation through the building, the bell rang and I was off to sit in my homeroom. She was there, too, but she managed to keep our friends.

Alone and awkward, I sat listening to the morning announcements. I stood with the rest of the class as we silently pledged our allegiance to the flag and waited for the next bell to send us to our first class. Homeroom was pointless. We didn't do anything for the ten minutes we were scheduled. I'd rather have gone straight to my first period class, which was French.

She walked past me with her friends out the door after the bell rang. I tried to get out first, but it was almost like she blocked me on purpose. We didn't lock eyes, but I heard her laugh and say my name as they continued down the hall. I wanted to cry, but I kept going the opposite direction to my classroom.

What did I do to deserve such treatment? Why couldn't I be a part of that group? What made me so different that I wasn't allowed to be included?

I really thought she and I were like twins. But how could we be, if one of us was accepted and the other wasn't?

My French class was a great distraction. We were really getting into culture, which meant watching films. It was a way to get my mind off my depressing affairs.

Lunch was going to be unbearable until my classmate and regular project partner, Charlie, asked to talk about our next presentation over lunch. It was nice to have someone to sit with, but I knew it wasn't going to be a permanent fixture. He had his own friends that he ignored today to sit with me.

When the final bell rang I felt my body robotically get up and make its way to the exit. No one stopped me to chat. No one asked if I wanted to hang out later. I walked through the sea of my peers and out the door, unnoticed.

When I got to my car, I let the tears fall. I turned up my music so no one could hear me as I rested my head on the steering wheel. People would think I was taking a nap.

I didn't think losing my best friend would mean losing all of my friends. I thought we were all close, but when push came to shove, they chose her side over mine. It didn't seem fair that I didn't get a say.

A knock on my window jolted me out of my misery and I locked eyes with Charlie. I quickly wiped my tears away and rolled down the window.

"Hey, are you okay?" Charlie asked with a concerned look as I continued to wipe my face.

"Yeah, I'm fine. Just got a bad score on a test. I'm fine." I tried to look cool in front of him. I went to roll up the window.

Charlie shook his head and placed his hand on the window to stop me. He wouldn't let it go.

"No... I know that's not right. Can you give me a ride? My mom can't pick me up. We can talk about what's bothering you."

Charlie quickly hopped into my car before I could answer and directed me towards his house.

"Girl, spill." He was still looking at me with concern.

"It's stupid." I shook my head trying to not seem so desperate for human connection.

"Lana, you have been in my class since kindergarten. We've grown up together... suffice it to say... I know you."

Charlie wouldn't look away from me, so I finally caved.

"So, the other day, Kayleigh decided we were no longer friends and the rest of my so-called friends walked out of my life with her."

"Shit. That's horrible, why?"

"Dude. I don't even know why."

Charlie gave me a look, "You know."

"The only thing I can think of was because I continued to host my bonfire night when she couldn't attend."

"Really?"

"Yeah! 'Cause the day after, she texted me and said I was a bitch for keeping the bonfire going and we weren't friends. I thought she was joking, but clearly not. Here look."

I grabbed my phone while we were at a stoplight and showed Charlie the messages. He scrolled through and shook his head. "So much high school drama. I can't wait until we go to college."

I nodded in agreement.

"Anyway, sounds like you need to take this negativity and just throw it behind you."

"Easier said, Chuck."

"Say that one more time, Laney."

We both laughed. It was refreshing to be with someone and not have to worry about saying the wrong thing.

"This is going to sound stupid, but Charlie, will you be my new friend?" I asked as I pulled onto his street.

"Lana, we're already friends. Just give me a call, whenever. If you don't mind hanging out with some gamers, I'm having a party on Friday. Come... don't worry there's no alcohol and my parents will be here."

"Cool, I'll see if I can come." Charlie nodded and hopped out of my car. Before he shut the door he ducked his head in.

"Life is so much more than the Kayleigh's of our school. See you tomorrow. Don't forget to write up that—"

"Research, yes Charlie. I'll do that tonight."

Charlie shut my door and I was left feeling better than I did coming into my car.

***

I wasn't sure what I was getting into when I entered Charlie's house for the first time. We always were partners in class, but we never really talked outside of school if it wasn't about the projects. I knew he was into computers and video games, but I wasn't entirely sure what "gamers" meant.

His mom answered the door, she recognized me from past award ceremonies, Charlie and I were always nominated/ appointed "Best" something for a subject. We were nerds.

"Lana, how nice to see you! You've grown so much."

"Yeah, thanks for having me over." I smiled awkwardly. She seemed really excited that I was there, and it made me wonder, was I the only girl?

"Well, Charlie and the rest are downstairs, I think they just started."

"Thanks." I walked towards the door where Charlie's mom pointed and made my way down. I heard some chatter and I started to feel really nervous. Would they like me?

I turned the corner and saw one of the girls in my math class; Elsie was jumping up and down on a pad with arrows, following the sequence shown on the TV in front of her. She locked eyes with me and waved.

"Hey! Lana's here!" she said before continuing the game.

"LANA!!" Everyone screamed my name as I turned the corner. Mike, another classmate of mine, handed me a can of coke.

"You have to get on our sugar level to play." He winked, "How'd you do on the Physics pop quiz? I'm trying to gauge if Mr. Drake will give us a curve."

"NO TALKING ABOUT GRADES, MIKE!" Elsie yelled as she made her finishing moves. The music stopped and a high score flashed on the screen. "Yes!"

"I was just trying to see if my F would become a D!"

I started laughing. I didn't feel nervous anymore; I felt at home. Elsie hopped over to me and placed her arm around my shoulder.

"It's cool to see you outside of school. I always thought you were like a super nerd who never went anywhere."

"No, up until recently she hung out with the *other* girls, but they kicked her out. Isn't that right, Lana?" Charlie smirked as he gulped his Mountain Dew.

"Yeah, pretty much."

"Such assholes! See, that's why I never spoke to them. They always seemed stuck up. Well, welcome, Lana, to the gamer crew. We are grateful for your attendance. And besides, I've always wanted have at least one more girl here!" Elsie laughed.

"So what are we playing?" I asked.

"You know what DDR is, right?"

"Yeah, they have that at gym. I never played though."

"Well, now's your time!" Mike took my coke away and pushed me onto the mat. "Just press the arrows that show up on the screen. Here, we'll put you on easy."

I didn't know what I was being forced into, but as soon as the music started and I pressed the right buttons, it was the beginning of the fun I had that night.

I never played games with my old friends. We always just sat around and talked about gossip or watched movies. If we weren't at home, then we were at the mall walking around and spending our parent's money.

The next game we played was Mario Kart. This game I knew because my younger brother, Josh, had this game. We would play together sometime whenever I wasn't busy spending time with Kayleigh. In fact, I was playing this with Josh the other night because I didn't have anything else to do after getting kicked to the curb.

I wasn't sure if I'd fit in with Charlie and his crew. I wasn't really a gaming person... but

I was open to learn and I think that's what made them like me.

"Yo! Lana was lying when she said she wasn't good at this game!" Mike tossed his remote to the floor as I took first place in the Grand Prix.

"Well, my little brother usually beats me..." I said nonchalantly.

"SHE JUST SAID YOU'RE WORSE THAN HER BROTHER, BRO!" Charlie yelled to Mike from the other side of the room. Mike waved Charlie off as he went to retrieve the remote he dropped.

"So, for real, how did you do on the test?" Mike asked quietly so the rest couldn't hear him.

"I probably got a 90 on it. So I wouldn't worry too much." I rolled my eyes. I actually think I got a perfect score, but I didn't want to sound like I was bragging.

"Cool. I didn't do so well... I read the wrong chapter. Like dude, who does that? Apparently me."

"Well, I could help you with extra credit if you need it."

Charlie entered the conversation carrying a plate of PB & J sandwiches.

"I hope you aren't talking about class... and that you aren't allergic to peanuts. I forgot to ask."

"No, I'm a huge peanut lover."

Mike and Charlie started chuckling and then I blushed with embarrassment.

"That's not what I meant..."

That sent Mike and Charlie into a huge laughing fit. Elsie and another guy, Jordan, walked over to see what was the commotion about.

"She said she's a HUGE peanut lover!" Mike said in between laughs. The others joined in with the laughter. I was so embarrassed but couldn't help and laugh myself.

I officially found new friends... and they were just as awkward as I was.

Going back to school after the weekend was still nerve wrecking, even though I felt that party was a success. No one had contacted me since. I was a little upset going into Sunday because I had thought maybe I wasn't good enough to be their friend.

Emi Sano

As I started to make my first round through the halls at my school I walked by Elsie who was trying to de-stuff her backpack in her locker. She caught sight of me and ran up beside me.

"Hey! How was your weekend?" Elsie asked, trying to zip up her bag before slinging it over her shoulder.

"It was quiet... I did homework and played with my little bro. You?"

"It was sooo boring! My parents decided that last weekend was no electronics weekend. Meaning, no phones, no TV, no computer! I had nothing to do... no one to talk to... except my parents of course. So I just read a book... okay two books..." Elsie bit her lip, "Fine it was five books. I was so fucking bored!"

I laughed as Elsie covered her face in embarrassment.

"I'm sorry for swearing."

"Why are you apologizing?"

"Oh, I just thought you didn't like people swearing." Elsie bit her lip nervously.

"What gave you that idea?"

"Because... you're you. Sweet innocent, Lana." Elsie gestured her hands around me as if she were putting me in an invisible box.

"What the fuck? Is that how people see me?"

"Whoa! She does swear!"

"Of course I swear. I'm not a prissy. I just don't do it in school." I mumbled the last part. I actually didn't swear at all, but it felt so good after saying it for the first time. "I didn't think people actually saw me as that."

"It's okay, we can help change that." Elsie wrapped her arm around my shoulder as we continued down the hall.

The homeroom bell rang.

"Hey, are you in second lunch?" Elsie asked quickly.

"Yeah."

"Great come sit with us by the stage. That is... if we're cool enough for you." Elsie smirked, egging me on.

"I don't know... if I'm cool enough for you guys."

Elsie rolled her eyes jokingly and walked off.

The whole time I was listening to the morning announcements I couldn't help but smile. It was the first time I felt happy, since being kicked out of my so-called "friend circle."

I didn't even care that Kayleigh and her posse were laughing in the corner about something. I didn't care that she kept throwing looks in my direction as we piled up to leave the room. I didn't care anymore, because it didn't bother me *anymore*.

I wasn't alone. I had *friends* and I cared about them more than what anyone thought about me.

The next few days I found out where the rest of the "gamer" crew hung out in the morning. It was so nice to not have to walk around school trying to fit in. I didn't even think about going into the school library to hang out.

I helped Mike on his physics classwork so he didn't fail physics class. Elsie would jump in during the tutoring session to comment on Mike's intelligence or lack thereof. Charlie and Jordan were too busy playing a game together on their phones. It was like we all have been friends for years. I was grateful for these guys accepting me into their group so quickly. I never expected people in my school to be this *nice*.

I asked Elsie why she hung out with a group of geeky guys one day.

She looked away before telling me. Her voice was softer than normal. It was almost like it embarrassed her. But she started chuckling before she spoke.

"I never got along with the *other* girls, you're the exception. The other girls didn't like the way I cut my hair or the way I played in recess. So I hung out with the boys and that's how I met Charlie. The other girls... they were so mean... you know? So, I just couldn't bring myself to be friends with any girl."

"Was I ever mean to you?"

"No, Lana. You weren't. Your friends were... but you weren't ever there when they did it. It's like they knew you wouldn't agree with what they did."

"I'm sorry... I wish I could've stopped them somehow."

"Dude, it's not your fault. And now that you're no longer friends with them you shouldn't have to carry that guilt."

I tried to smile with Elsie, but it was hard knowing I might have caused her pain. I remember Kayleigh talking crap about Elsie when we were younger. I never spoke up about it. I wish I had.

At lunch it was a bunch of nerds and geeks just nerding and geeking out with each other. It was like we were in our own little world. Charlie was trying to teach me how to play a card game called Magic. I was just about to beat him when Kayleigh had to come crashing into our bubble like Godzilla.

"Wow... Lana... I didn't think you'd go find friends in such a low... dirty place." Kayleigh was standing behind me. I had to turn around to look at her. She wasn't alone, the rest of her posse were standing behind her as well.

"What the fuck are you talking about, Kay?"

"Wow. So I see you're still willing to change for new friends. You haven't *changed* one bit."

"Why are you even talking to me?" I asked her as I stood up. I saw Elsie clenching her fists beside me. I put my hand out to stop her.

"I was just curious... I heard you already moved on and I wanted to see what stupid group let you in. I should have known. Nerds stick together."

"We're geeks. Not nerds," Jordan snorted.

"Well, I'm a nerd, too," Charlie piped in and shrugged when Jordan shot him a look.

"Whatever! You guys are anti-social freaks! Lana... are you sure you want to be seen around these people? Think about how your senior year is going to be like. Don't you want to go to parties?"

"Not with you! And I don't give a shit about the senior year of bull. We're all going off to college – well some of us are – and we might not see each other again until the ten, twenty, fifty year reunion! I wouldn't mind if I ever saw you again."

Kayleigh's mouth dropped. It was oddly satisfying to watch her posse crumbling as well.

"And, Kayleigh, while we're on the subject. Yes, those jeans you bought did make your ass look fat. And those highlights in your hair are extremely tacky. I also hate the way you sing. You're so tone deaf, but the rest of your friends are too afraid to tell you. If you're here trying to make me beg to be your friend again, it's not going to work. I'm better off with friends who actually give a damn about my thoughts and respect me as a person."

I looked over at her posse, "And if you guys actually had a backbone, you wouldn't be standing behind her either."

Kayleigh looked at her friends who were sort of cowering in fear from her anger. She whipped her eyes back to me and stared me down for a brief second before walking off.

"So, I'm thinking of throwing a bonfire this weekend, anyone game? We also have a hot tub..." I said loud enough for Kayleigh to hear. I knew she did because I saw her glare at me out of the corner of my eye.

It felt so good.

No, it felt so *fucking* good.

CALEB

"HE'S MY SON! THAT BOY DESERVES TO BE IN HELL!" Sam's father exclaimed. Fortunately, his mother was more kind-spirited; despite the fact the accident killed her only child.

"We and John's parents have already grieved enough about losing our boys... and Caleb's mom has been with us since the accident. I would not be able to stand myself if I was the reason for her losing Caleb. Hank, it was an accident. Just accept it." I heard her say before she walked away.

All this shouting took place in front of me, not literally, but I could still hear it. I was in my hospital bed still recovering from my five broken ribs, fractured arm, and road burns galore and Sam's parents were standing outside door. Hank took one look at me and saw red. I didn't blame him. After all, his son was dead because of me.

Hank didn't want to have anything to do with me after that. I wasn't allowed to be at the wake or funeral of my best friend. He couldn't accept that his son died as a result of a nasty car wreck.

John's parents didn't react the same way. They took care of me at the hospital while my mom was at work. I was like their second child, and they were thrilled that at least I had survived. I think everyone knew that since my father died in Iraq my mom has been in a fragile state of mind. It was hard on the both of us, but I think she took it the worst. And my accident didn't help, of course.

The whole accident was a blur. I don't remember much what happened during and after. All I remember was that we were laughing and something jumped out in front of me on the road and I swerved. The next thing I woke up in the hospital and in pain. I thought it was the worst pain I have ever felt... but then I found out that I killed my two best friends.

I cried for hours. I didn't want to take any pain medication. I refused the morphine drip until my mom forcibly took the button away from my fingers and pushed it for me. I deserved to be in pain. I deserved to die too.

That's how I felt, anyway. But then I saw the look in my mom's eyes as she watched me struggle between life and death. It was the same look that she gave me when she had to tell me my dad died on a mission in Iraq. I didn't even know he was in Iraq. He never told me where he was going, only that he was just going to protect us. When she gave me that look, I knew that I had to toughen up and stay alive... not for me, but for her.

After I got out of the hospital, I wasn't allowed to go back to school for another week. The doctors wanted me to go to physical therapy and give my burns a chance to heal. I was fine with the idea of staying at home. I worried what it would be like if I went back to school. I didn't know if other people thought the same thing Sam's father did, that I was a murderer.

My mom wouldn't let me on social media the whole time I was recovering. She felt that some kids would be cruel and would push back my recovery process. I didn't disagree, but it did kill me that I couldn't check in on how everyone was doing. Besides, the only people I wanted to talk to anyway were dead.

I woke up every morning drenched in sweat. I think I was having nightmares about the accident, but I never remembered any of them. It was like my brain was trying to force me to remember what happened. I didn't want to. I liked having it be black whenever I tried to remember. It was bad enough seeing that stupid raccoon in the middle of the road over and over again.

John's parents would come by the house every now and then. They talked about his funeral arrangements... how it was separate from Sam's. In the end Sam's family decided to keep the funeral within the family and not let any of the friends come to pay their respects. I felt like they were being selfish, but I didn't express my thoughts. Maybe I was being selfish for wanting to say goodbye to the friend that I killed.

Unlike Sam's, John's mass and wake were going to be open to the public. His parents reassured me that I was allowed to attend and they'd do their best to make sure no one came after me while I was there. They wanted me to be a part of their family, to stand by the casket when he was being lowered. I told them that it didn't feel right, but I thanked them for inviting me and I promised that I would come to the mass and wake.

The funeral mass was hard to get through. Not only was I awkwardly sitting with my itchy arm in the cast, but I also felt like the mass was directed towards me. The whole time the priest was talking about redemption and how God will bring judgment in the end. He kept mentioning that all John's sins would be forgiven. I cried at that part. I wondered if it were true. Would I be forgiven? Would God accept me in His home even though I killed my best friends?

Everyone at the wake avoided me. I figured this would happen. My mom was too busy talking with John's parents, trying to take her mind off things and also making sure they were okay. It was tough for my mom to be at the funeral so soon after my dad died. I thought she never wanted to attend another funeral again. I was surprised that she was okay with coming along to John's. But then again, we were all so close... it was like he was a part of her family as well.

Sam's mother showed up to the wake. It was weird and awkward when she came up to me. She took me into her arms and held me tight. I wanted to squirm away, but I let her hold me as long as she needed. I guess she never really got the opportunity to express her gratitude that I survived.

"How are you holding up?" she asked as she finally let go of me.

"I'm hanging in there. Surviving... for them."

"I'm sure Sam would appreciate that. He always said you were going to go far in life." She chuckled. A wave of sadness came across her face before returning back to normal.

"Mrs. Bakersfield..."

"Don't... you're alive. That's all that matters. Okay? Don't let Hank's outburst the other day haunt you. We all want you to grow. We all want you to succeed. Don't say another word. You hear?"

I nodded. She was always the tough mom out of all our moms. Sam was also like her. He knew he wasn't smart enough, but he was always the one to back us up. He was our personal cheerleader and always made sure that we felt better about ourselves.

I stood above the casket. It was closed. John was too mangled, they said. I wondered if he felt any pain. I cried so many times that day. No one else came to the casket while I stood there.

"I'm so sorry, bud. I'm so sorry," I said over and over again. My tears flooded down my cheeks. I was practically on top of the casket when John's mother walked up and pulled me away.

The longer I stayed at the wake, the more I wanted to just crawl into a hole and never come out. My worst fears about school were coming true. I had glares sent in my direction from some of my classmates. Others were looking at me in pity. No one would talk to me, though. Not one person came up to say hi. I wondered if I needed to change schools.

My mom came to my rescue as she pulled me out of the funeral hall. She reminded me that the burial was going to be a private viewing. She felt we had been there long enough. I'd gotten the chance to say my goodbye, so I really was glad to get out of there.

It was hard not being able see John's face. I wanted to really look at him and tell him face to face how sorry I was. I don't know if that would have made me feel any better. I never got any type of closure with Sam.

When the doctors finally cleared me to go to school, my road burns were healed and but the scars remained. I looked like a monster.

It was like being at the wake all over again. Everyone was just staring as I walked past. Some were too pissed to talk, some too scared. Either way, it was maddening. I felt like screaming at everyone.

"JUST SAY SOMETHING!" I wanted to shout. I wanted them to break the silence. It was deafening. Even the teachers didn't know what to say. They all avoided me like I had cancer. Actually, I would be treated better if I had cancer. I didn't care if they said something mean to me either. I just wanted someone to say anything just so I didn't feel like the center of a freak show.

Ali was a girl that was really close friends with John. I saw her at the wake. She was the only one who actually smiled at me as we locked eyes at John's wake. She didn't speak with me then, but I had a feeling her friends were holding her back.

I saw Ali at lunch; we were standing next to each other in line. Ali looked back and when she saw me she immediately gave me a hug. I groaned because I was still healing in my ribcage. Ali looked up at me with tears in her eyes.

"It's just awful, the whole thing, Caleb. I'm so sorry you had to go through that." Ali wiped away her tears.

"Thanks..." I trailed off, not knowing how to respond.

Ali shook her head, "No, the things they're saying about you too. I wanted you to hear it from me first. Don't listen to what they call you, okay? You're a survivor. You're lucky."

"What have they been saying?" I asked and instantly regretted it.

"They've been calling you a friend killer."

"Well, they're not lying..."

"Caleb! It was a freak accident. You didn't do it on purpose." Ali shook her head as the line continued towards the food counter.

"Ali, why are you talking to me right now?"

"I felt bad... at John's wake. I didn't say anything to you then... and I couldn't reach out to you online... I just... wanted to say that I'm sorry."

"I'm sorry, too. I know how much you liked John."

"Was it that obvious? He didn't even know."
Ali blushed, new tears forming in her eyes.
"Anyway, you can sit with me, okay? I don't
want you to be alone."

"I'm not suicidal."

"I don't care."

After that conversation, Ali and I shared
lunch every day. It was almost like life had
returned to some normalcy. Sure, I still got the
stares, but it went away with each passing day.
Soon people forgot that John and Sam were
gone. They were too worried about midterms.

I didn't forget them, though. It was hard
not to. They were my best friends; they were
my brothers. They were the ones I'd go to
whenever I had good news. When I got my
midterms back and I got that impossible B+ in
Trigonometry I wanted to run to Sam's locker
to show him. But Sam wasn't there and he
wouldn't be there anymore.

When the baseball team was posted, they
made an honorary position for John. He was an
okay baseball player. He wasn't going to go to
the big leagues or anything. But he did have a
pretty solid batting average. John would have

laughed if he saw that. He would have rolled his eyes and hid in embarrassment. He didn't like getting attention like that.

Every time I felt like I had made some progress, I always felt a pang of guilt come along with it. People called it survivor's guilt. I never understood what that meant until now.

Each day that I was alive, I was growing and learning. I was achieving goals and succeeding... but they weren't. They were stuck at 16 years old.

Forever young. Forever gone. But never forgotten.

I would live every day in their honor, in their name, until the day I die. That's the only way I'll be able to make it through life without them by my side.

LIFE

ANNA

ANNA WAS SHORT, BONEY, AND IN NO WAY LOOKED LIKE ANY OF THE BASKETBALL PLAYERS ON HER TEAM. She was passionate about the game and practiced harder to be a part of it.

She was so excited at the end of her sophomore year of high school when her varsity coach, Mr. Martin, all but promised her a spot on the team next year. He said he was very impressed by her dedication. This filled her with hope for the next season.

Then, word came out that the Mr. Martin was to be fired because some of the parents of her teammates complained about unfair playing time. Anna was saddened by the news, but still hopeful that her varsity dreams weren't going to be crushed.

The new coach that replaced Mr. Martin was none other than her mom's archenemy, Mrs. Conley. She and Anna's mom were in the same class and Mrs. Conley hated her for stealing her boyfriend... and then later on marrying him.

Years ago, when Anna was working her way up in the recreation league, Mrs. Conley refused to have her on her team. She was one of the good coaches in the league and Anna's mom was royally pissed off that Mrs. Conley still held a grudge, so she started coaching Anna herself.

Anna told her mom about Mrs. Conley's new position at the school and relayed her fears that she wouldn't make the varsity team.

"It's been over 20 years. I'm sure she's over it by now. Don't worry, your skills will show in tryouts and she'll have to pick you to be on the team."

Anna tried to agree with her mom, but she had her doubts. At tryouts, Anna couldn't help but feel that she was being pushed more than the other girls. Mrs. Conley yelled at Anna more and criticized her for every single thing she did. At the end of the week, Anna was sure that she was going to be put on Junior Varsity again while the rest of her classmates advanced to Varsity.

The day the team list was posted, Anna slowly made her way through the girls who were crying or high-fiving each other. When she read the Varsity list she nearly died.

Her name was posted as the last person: Anna Matthews – Guard. She quickly texted her mom the news and they celebrated that night.

But the season didn't go as well as she thought. Despite being drilled hard at practice, Anna never got any playing time. Her mom took it to the Athletic Director, but he said it was out of his hands; there were no complaints about Mrs. Conley from other parents so he didn't see that it was a necessary issue.

Anna was frustrated towards the end of the season. How would she be able to get a college scholarship if she couldn't play a single game? The thought weighed heavy on Anna all through practice. One afternoon, Mrs. Conley scolded her from across the gym for not running hard enough.

"What's the point, coach? You'll never put me in the game anyway!" Anna fired back.

Mrs. Conley got red in the face and pulled Anna aside, "I will never put you in the game with that attitude! Don't bother trying out next year, because I won't even put you on the roster."

Anna held back hot tears and went back to the running drills with the rest of her teammates. One of them, Melissa, ran up to her and asked if she was okay. Anna just shook her head in response but didn't tell her what Mrs. Conley said.

At the end of the season, Anna had two minutes of total playing time. She was put in for the last thirty seconds of the last four games because they were losing anyway and weren't going to make the playoffs. Three other freshmen girls had more playing time than she, a junior, did. This devastated Anna.

What was going to be her life now? All she had was basketball. She quit every other extra-curricular because they interfered with basketball; there was no way they'd take her back now.

Senior year was supposed to be her shining year. She'd play varsity and get to show off during Senior Night with the rest of her class. Anna dreamt of that night ever since she watched her cousins play theirs. All of that came crashing down when she saw the tryouts posting on the bulletin board.

Anna knew she wouldn't make the team. The varsity coach was still Mrs. Conley. The rest of her teammates quickly wrote their names on the sign up sheet and when they saw Anna walk away, they bombarded her with questions.

"Why aren't you trying out? It's our senior year!"

"I know last year sucked, but you'll still make the team!"

"Come on, Anna, we need you. You know the plays better than any of us."

Anna stopped in her steps and turned to her teammates who were all desperate to have her on their team. "Mrs. Conley said she wouldn't put me on the team, anyway. I should just focus on my education."

Their mouths agape, they didn't follow Anna as she continued to her classroom. After the first day of tryouts, Melissa came to Anna and told her that Mrs. Conley said she'd give her a second chance if she tried out. Anna laughed and shook her head; she wasn't in any condition to play anyway. She stopped training after the last season.

"Thanks for asking, though. I'll be okay," Anna said. Melissa looked crushed as she turned back in her seat.

When the first game came, Anna felt alone. She loved dressing up for the games and carrying her duffel bag around with her. It had made her feel important, like she was a valuable part of the team.

As she watched as her old teammates pile onto the bus to go off to their first game, she wanted to cry. She regretted not trying out; maybe Mrs. Conley would've let her play.

Anna's mom told her to stop reflecting on the past and try to find something to keep her occupied. Anna wasn't really in the mood to listen to her mom, but she tried her best to follow the advice.

At school, Anna tried to not let her mind wander to the game, no matter how many times she heard or saw her teammates talk about it. One of her non-basketball friends, Chelsea, asked what she was thinking of doing in college.

"I never really thought about it. I was going to try and get a scholarship through basketball at UNC, but that's out of the question now." Anna slumped in her chair.

Chelsea laughed, "You can still go to UNC!"

Anna smiled at the thought, but she never really had any ideas on what her career would be.

"I always imagined you going into Marketing. Mr. Hamill loved having you in class. He still talks about you and your wins at DECA." Chelsea shook her head, "I think he wished there were more marketing courses you could have taken so he could keep you on the team."

"Really? I never really thought about that. I do like advertising..." Anna trailed off, thinking about her future without basketball. For the first time in months she was feeling hopeful. "You know what, I'll start looking at colleges with that in mind."

With the process of applying to colleges, Anna had zero time to be reflecting on basketball and how she missed it. *This was better for me*, she thought. Looking forward to her future and career goals replaced that high she got when she played.

By the end of the season, Anna had been accepted to four colleges and was attempting to narrow down her decision. One of the main concerns for her was financial affordability, but thanks to Mr. Hamill, she was able to get a lot of enthusiastic letters of recommendation written for her with scholarship programs that aimed towards young girls going into business.

Anna received enough financial grants and scholarships to afford going to her dream school, University of North Carolina.

Even as she was filling out her housing placement survey, she was still in shock that this was all happening. Anna was still going to be a Tar Heel, just not as a basketball player. Even though she wasn't going to play basketball at UNC, she will still be attending the games and cheering them on. When graduation came along, Mrs. Conley was there to give a speech about perseverance and how she was proud of this year's group of seniors. Afterwards, she had stopped Anna and her mom on the way to the parking lot.

"Anna, I want to apologize for what I had said last year. I really was hoping to see you at tryouts."

Anna's mom was about to step in and tear Mrs. Conley a new one, but Anna stopped her before she could.

"It's okay, I realized that basketball wasn't as important as I thought it was. You helped me see that. Good luck, I hope we can finally win a divisional." Anna smiled as she walked away with her mom.

"I can't tell if that was an insult..." Anna's mom chuckled as she wrapped her arm around Anna.

"I don't know... she can take it however she wants." Anna smiled.

Anna and her family piled into their car. Anna looked out the window as they were pulling away from her high school. She was looking forward to trying new experiences at college.

JULIE

JULIE WOKE UP IN HER MESSY APARTMENT TO THE BLINDING SUNLIGHT SHINING THROUGH HER LIVING ROOM WINDOW. She had fallen asleep on her couch, again. She rolled her legs off the cushions and let her feet hit the floor. Her joints groaned in agony from being on the couch for ten hours.

Her cellphone rang for the umpteenth time with several texts from her overbearing mother checking in on her. Julie texted her mom that everything was fine and she was getting ready to head into work.

Her apartment hadn't been the same since Mike took off. Julie had found out he was cheating on her with his co-worker and instead of admitting it, he grabbed some of his belongings and bounced. Julie came home from work seeing her apartment in a mess and a note saying:

I can't. Bye.

- M

It took her a week to be able to go back to work. Luckily, she had paid time off and an understanding boss. This day marked a month since he left. Julie actually felt better going to work and being around friends, but returning home was like returning to a crime scene. She knew that she needed to clean and get rid of things that reminded her of Mike. She knew that making her apartment her own would make her feel better, but she didn't have the motivation to start. Every time she tried, she would feel overwhelmed and start to cry. She felt pathetic, grieving over a boyfriend.

Julie worked for an online magazine as one of the senior contributors. When she walked into the office there was a small crowd of people looking into a conference room. Julie wasn't sure what was going on, so she joined.

"Hey, why are we all standing here?" Julie asked as she approached the group.

"It's Adopt-a-thon Day! Look! They have dogs and cats!" Sheila exclaimed as she moved so Julie could see. "I told John I might bring home one of these babies, but he forbade me."

Casey, one of Julie's closest friends at work, joined the group. "Julie, you should totally take one home."

"Ha, yeah, Mike was allergic so I could never think about it." Julie watched as a pit bull mix rolled on his back looking for belly rubs from one the handlers. "Who is covering this?"

"You are!" Sheila smiled, "We all wanted to—well Morty didn't want to— so Lance pulled a name out of a hat and it was yours!"

"We were just waiting for you to come in." Casey smiled, too. Casey knew this would be good for Julie. She has watched her mental state decline after Mike left. Casey felt terrible that she couldn't pull Julie out of the funk, but was always there for every crying shoulder event.

Julie stepped into the conference room and greeted the handlers and volunteers from the rescue. The photographer, Lauren, had already set up the area for pictures.

"Thanks for coming in. I'm Julie; I'll be writing this piece."

"We love doing this with you guys! Can you believe that we get more adoptions, not just with the ones we highlight, but others as well?" April, the head of the rescue, hugged Dobby, the tabby cat, as she spoke.

"Yeah, I've been thinking of adopting a dog myself."

"We could start you up on an application when we're done! We'll do a house check and get you a pup!"

"House check?" Julie asked as she sat down in her chair to take notes.

"Yes, we have to make sure your home will be good for our dogs. We don't want them to come back, if we can't help it."

Julie thought back to her messy apartment and winced. She was definitely not ready for a dog.

April saw her hesitation and laughed, "Don't worry, we aren't looking for cleanliness. Just making sure they won't escape or get into any chemicals."

Julie sighed with relief. The pit bull mix she saw earlier asking for belly rubs came up to her and rested his head on her lap. Julie smiled and started petting his soft head.

"Baxter. He's three years old, been with us for a year. We've put him with a foster because he couldn't handle the stress at the kennel. Poor guy, he was given to us because his owner had a baby."

Baxter looked up at Julie with his sad eyes.

"Why hasn't he been adopted? He seems really calm and sweet."

"People are still leery of pit bulls." April took Baxter's leash. "Let's get him pictured first. Here's his info card."

Julie started typing up the info on her laptop. She watched as Baxter posed sweetly for the pictures. The rest of the animals were just as sweet and in need of loving homes. Being around them made Julie forget about her sad state at home. After the shoot, April handed Julie the application.

"You don't have to decide on a specific dog or cat yet. We can keep your application on file and when you're ready we will be able to process the adoption quickly." April smiled as Baxter ran up to Julie and placed his head on her lap again.

"I think Baxter wants to adopt me," Julie joked. She gave Baxter a kiss on the nose. "Can I fill this out now and give it to you?"

"Yes! We're going to start loading up the animals, but I'll wait for you." April left Baxter with Julie as she directed her volunteers. Baxter laid down on Julie's feet as she filled out the application. Already, she felt at ease. It was amazing how one dog could lift her mood. She secretly hoped he wouldn't be adopted right away.

When Julie went home the feeling of dread didn't wash over her as it normally did. She took it as a sign to get started on cleaning the house. If she wanted to bring Baxter here she wanted him to have a clean home. Julie knew she couldn't do it on her own, so she called for back up. Casey came over with a bottle of wine and her cleaning supplies. Julie didn't think she deserved a friend like Casey, but was happy to have her.

Casey and Julie threw out and reorganized everything in the apartment while holding on to a buzz from the wine. When they had finished, it was well into the night and they were done with the second bottle (Casey had to run out and buy a second one halfway through.)

Together, they sat on the couch Julie woke up on that very morning.

"You will not sleep on this couch tonight... because I'm sleeping on this couch." Casey hiccuped and they both laughed.

"Yes, ma'am." Julie leaned her head against the armrest. "Do you think I'm doing this right?"

"A dog can't cheat on you," Casey said directly.

"Yeah, but what if I get too busy at work and I can't take care of him."

Casey gave Julie a look. "Girl, you know you could bring him to work."

"I forgot about that..." Julie thought for a minute, "What if I'm really horrible at taking care of him?"

"Stop making excuses..." Casey yawned.

"There's got to be a reason."

"Huh?"

Julie started to cry, "There's got to be a reason why he left me..."

"Julie... he's a dick. You know he's a dick. You deserve happiness and if that dog is going to make you happy, then get the dog." Casey yawned again. "Now, stiffen up that upper lip and get yourself to bed. We're going to the rescue center tomorrow before he's adopted."

Julie wiped away her tears and hugged Casey tight before dragging her drunk self into bed.

* * *

At the rescue center, April was manning the welcome desk when Julie and Casey walked in.

"Julie! I'm so happy to see you. Have you decided to adopt?"

"Yes, I heard the article generated quite an interest." Julie smiled. Casey linked arms with her.

"Julie is too nervous to ask. Is Baxter still here?"

April's eyes lit up and nodded her head. "I've actually asked his foster to bring him in today. Sounds like fate, huh? He's in the playroom. Come with me."

Julie couldn't help but feel anxious. This was going to be a lifetime commitment. Something, she had thought, would be trying to thwart it from happening, like with Mike.

Baxter immediately greeted Julie with kisses. It was like he remembered her. April and Casey both left Julie alone with him. Julie sat on the floor and Baxter immediately lay down beside her, resting his head on her lap. Julie's eyes filled with tears, she felt an overwhelming sensation of joy. Baxter looked up at Julie and their eyes locked. His tail wagged faster. He quickly jumped up and began licking her tears off her cheeks. It was at this moment Julie knew she couldn't leave him there.

April was delighted to see Baxter finally getting his forever home. She scheduled the home inspection and promised Baxter will be Julie's if she passed. Julie was worried that the inspection would be the thing to block her from getting Baxter, but when the inspection day came April was overjoyed about how well the apartment looked. Julie took a sigh of relief.

Baxter was finally hers, forever.

The first night was rough. Baxter cried all night and so did Julie. She knew he was missing his foster mom. She didn't know how to make it easier for him. So, together, they slept on the couch.

By the end of the first week, her and Baxter finally got into rhythm. Baxter slept on Mike's side of the bed, filling the hole that was left behind. Julie was forced to go outside more, because Baxter loved walks. Instead of going on the couch after work, Julie would take Baxter to the park and let him run around with other dogs.

Casey would join them on the walks and was impressed with the overall mood change of Julie's.

"A couple years ago, if you would have said that I'd see you out hiking on the weekends, I would have laughed." Casey joked as they walked down a trail with Baxter happily walking ahead of them.

"Yeah, I know. I don't know why I've never done this before. I kind of like this."

"See, I told you this was a good idea."

"Yes, you did. Thank you, for everything. I mean it. I've never been happier." Julie smiled as she watched Baxter happily sniff around.

"Have you... heard from him at all?"

"Mike? No. The last contact was that note. He un-friended me and never returned any of my calls."

Baxter started barking at something in front of him. Someone screamed.

"Baxter! Come!" Baxter growled some more before he followed Julie's command.

Casey and Julie caught up to where Baxter was and to her surprise, it was Mike.

"Speak of the devil..." Casey said under her breath.

"You?"

"You got a dog?"

"Who is this, Mike?"

Everyone spoke at the same time. It almost felt as the world begun to spin for Julie as she took a step back. She hadn't seen his co-worker. Only read the text messages they sent each other. She looked like everything that Julie wasn't.

"Julie, what are you doing out here? You don't go on hikes! Is this your dog?" Mike was as astounded to see Julie as she was to see him.

Casey was holding Baxter back, who clearly knew that Mike was affecting his mom in a bad way.

"I-I did. I just got him a month ago. I didn't know you liked going on hikes?" Julie was looking at his hiking gear. The hydro-pack he was wearing and his newly bought hiking boots.

"Mike?" The girl standing beside him was starting to look annoyed.

"I think we should keep moving." Casey was starting to have trouble keeping Baxter at bay.

Julie took control of Baxter and they continued walking. Casey followed behind.

Julie looked behind her and noticed Mike's girl was crossing her arms in anger.

"Casey, I think we just ruined his date."

"Good. He deserves it." Casey laughed.

Julie shook her head as she pat Baxter on his head. Baxter gave her a couple licks on the hand. She instantly felt calmer.

"Well, for one thing, I'm glad I have Baxter now. Mike will never stop by."

They both laughed together as Baxter happily continued to run off and smell the woods in front of them.

That night, Baxter and Julie lie together on the bed. Baxter had his head on the unused pillow beside her. His eyes were closed and he was breathing heavily while his paws moved in a running formation. Julie watched all this going on and felt lucky.

Two months ago, she was down out of her luck. She lost her boyfriend, someone she dreamed to be her future husband, and wasn't sure what she was going to do with life after.

Now, she had this wonderful creature she shared a bed with and couldn't be any happier.

Emi Sano

Baxter woke up and licked his lips. His eyes were still groggy from being asleep but when he noticed Julie was looking at him his ears perked up and tail wagged under the blanket. He stretched out his neck and started licking Julie's nose.

Julie imagined he was thinking the same thing.

AMELIA

AMELIA FOLLOWED BABA DOWN BRIGHTLY LIT AISLES OF THE GROCERY STORE. She helped grab items her grandmother couldn't reach. Amelia was too small herself, but she was light enough to climb the shelves without breaking them. Sometimes she wondered if that was the only reason why Baba took her grocery shopping. Her older brother, Ken, never went grocery shopping with her grandmother and he could reach the shelves just as easily.

Amelia didn't mind it though; it was their special time together.

The only thing that bothered her most while they were out grocery shopping was the looks that other people gave them as they meandered through the aisles.

Baba was a 4 foot 11 inches tall, sixty-five-year-old Japanese woman, whose no-nonsense mentality showed through her face in a permanent scowl. Her dark hair bounced above her shoulders as she walked a slow gait.

Amelia looked like a younger and sunnier version of Baba especially with her short hair. Her brown eyes lit up whenever she smiled, which was all the time. She was only six years old, but her mind was like one twice her age.

Amelia often noticed the daggers coming out of the people's eyes whenever Baba walked by. She wondered why they were so angry. Amelia never asked her grandmother about it; she was too afraid.

At the register, Baba had Amelia help put all the groceries on the belt while she told the cashier what carton of cigarettes to grab for her husband. The red and white box was swiped across the scanner and thrown into the bag.

"Your total comes to $89.32."

"Okay, one second." Baba said as she opened her checkbook to write out the check.

Amelia could hear the annoyed sighs behind them. She looked back and saw the people in line watching Baba with irritated looks on their faces.

"How much?" Baba asked.

"Eight. Nine. Three. Two." The cashier responded slowly to Baba. The cashier rolled her eyes and tapped her fingers on the belt, waiting.

Amelia watched as Baba shook her head while she wrote out the check. She couldn't understand why everyone seemed so impatient with her grandmother.

Baba wasn't stupid. She was the smartest woman Amelia knew – aside from her mom of course. Baba was short with her words, but she always spoke with wisdom that was sometimes beyond Amelia's understanding.

With a quick *rip,* Baba tore out the check and gave it the woman. The cashier wordlessly handed her the receipt.

"Thank you. Bye-bye," Baba said as she shoved the receipt into her purse and gestured for Amelia to help push the cart. Amelia instantly obeyed and began following behind Baba to the parking lot.

Back at her grandparent's house, Amelia sat on her grandpa's chair watching some cartoons that Baba put on while she started to make an afternoon snack.

Her grandpa came home from picking up Ken from school.

"Grandpa!" Amelia shouted as she ran up to give him a hug. Compared to Baba, Grandpa was a 6 foot 2 inches giant. Amelia felt like an ant standing next to him. She always liked the way Grandpa's blue eyes lit up whenever he smiled. They were the same color as the sky when the sun was up high.

"Hey there, ladybug. Did you do anything fun today?" Grandpa picked Amelia up and carried her in his arms.

"Went grocery shopping."

"Did you get to climb any shelves?"

"Yeah!" Amelia smiled, but quickly faded. "Grandpa... why are the people at the store so mean to Baba?"

"Oh, they're just grumpy people. Never you mind. Now go and finish the show. I'll be back." Grandpa put Amelia back down and Ken joined Amelia in the living room to watch the show.

Ken was in the fourth grade and their parents were constantly talking about how proud they were that he skipped a grade. They always told people that he was too smart for his age and he would probably become a doctor.

Amelia couldn't wait until next year when she could start first grade. She was tired of watching Ken get all the praises. Amelia knew she could be just as smart as Ken and hoped that she would skip a grade too... as soon as she found out what that meant.

"This show is stupid." Ken remarked as he went to change the channel from the fairy princess show.

"No! I was watching it!" Amelia shrieked. Ken gave her the same look the people at the grocery store gave Baba. Amelia shrunk. "Fine."

Ken smiled and he changed the channel to another cartoon. It was an old cartoon and to Ken it was more funny.

Amelia pouted and left the room. She entered the kitchen where Grandpa and Baba were talking in hushed tones. Amelia stood back and watched.

"It's nothing, *just the usual racism*. I'm used to this by now," Baba said as she was finishing cutting the carrots.

"Amelia saw it. You have to speak up for yourself." Grandpa placed a hand on Baba's arm.

"And say what? Just because I am Japanese don't mean I am stupid? I have an accent, but I speak English? Stop looking at me? You know that won't change." Baba refused to look up from the carrots.

Amelia continued into the room, pretending like she didn't hear anything, "Baba, Ken changed the channel."

"Oh, let him get to watch what he wants. You had your time today." Baba shooed Amelia back into the living room. Grandpa followed her out.

Amelia felt safe with Grandpa. She felt like she could ask him anything and he'd always know the answer.

With Baba, she always said, "Ask your mother."

Grandpa sat in his chair and Amelia immediately climbed on top of his lap. She curled up against his warm body.

"Grandpa..."

"Yes, bug?"

"What's *racism*?"

"It's when people don't like other people because of the who they are."

"Why don't people like Baba?"

"Oh Amelia, some people are just too grumpy." Grandpa tried to change the subject. "Don't go worrying over something like that, it makes your smile go away."

"They don't like Baba because she looks different," Ken said from where he was sitting.

"But mama says I look like Baba... so does that mean people don't like me?" Amelia's eyes started to water.

Grandpa shot a look at Ken, who instantly cowered.

"Bug, don't worry about that, everyone loves you."

Ken snorted and continued to watch the television.

Amelia couldn't help but let a few tears fall onto her cheeks. She didn't understand why people would hate Baba and hate her too.

Grandpa hugged Amelia extra tight, and she instantly felt safe again. But then he set her down on the floor and got up from the chair.

"Ken," that was all Grandpa had to say and it was enough to bring Ken to his feet and follow Grandpa upstairs.

"Don't you dare tell your sister that again," Grandpa's harsh voice carried down the stairwell. Amelia stood at the bottom of the stairs, frozen. She never heard Grandpa talk like that before and it was terrifying.

"The kids at the school already make fun of me for being different! She's going to get the same treatment. We can't treat her like a baby forever," Ken shouted back at Grandpa.

"She's only six years old. She doesn't understand. All she thinks now is that everyone hates her and Baba."

Amelia heard Ken sniffle.

"I... she has to know before she starts school... that everyone isn't gonna be nice." Ken's voice trailed off. His sobs muffled.

"I know..." Grandpa's voice softened back to his usual tone.

Baba came to Amelia's side and nearly frightened her.

"Amelia, come let's have a snack."

Amelia turned and looked at Baba whose face was more gentle and kinder than it was at the store.

"Okay." Amelia took Baba's hand and walked over to the table.

She ate a few carrots in silence with Baba. After a couple moments Amelia finally spoke.

"Baba... why do people hate us?"

"Who said that?"

"Ken."

"People don't hate us. They are jealous. We look different. We are unique. That is why people stare. Not hate. Just jealous." Baba nodded. "Ken don't understand. Ken is still a young boy."

Amelia bit her lip and then smiled, "Okay."

Ken walked in the room followed by Grandpa. His eyes were red and puffy from crying and Baba's eyes flit to Grandpa in anger. Grandpa put his hands up in defense.

"Ken... Baba says people are jealous of us, they don't hate us," Amelia said.

Ken looked at Baba and then to his sister. "Yeah, I guess she's right."

Amelia nodded with a big smile. "I like being different."

"Me, too." Baba said.

Amelia's mind was put at ease for the rest of the day. She felt happy knowing she knew something before Ken did.

Not only that, she also learned not to make Grandpa angry.

MISSY

MISSY WOKE UP TO THE SAME ROUTINE EVERYDAY.

Her watch vibrated on her wrist to wake her up. She crawled out of her makeshift bed as she made her way through her shack of a house. Everything was either war-torn or scavenged. Her tiny kitchen/bathroom had a sink, a hot plate, and a toilet. The toilet and sink were the two things that still worked when she found this place. To her surprise, someone had left. It was almost pure luck that she was able to make this her new home.

Her watch vibrated on her wrist again, this time it wasn't an alarm, it was to notify her of someone's presence. She set up security points throughout the perimeter. If someone tricked the silent alarm, she'd know. Her watch said north point was triggered.

Missy put down her cup of water and grabbed her shotgun she had found along her journey. She checked the ammo and made her way to the tiny window that faced the north side of the shack.

There wasn't anyone there. Either someone had triggered it by walking by, or they made their way to the door.

Her watch vibrated again. She looked down and it notified her of the south point trigger.

Great. Missy had managed to stay alive this long on her own. She didn't want to die now.

Her watch vibrated: Speech detected.

Missy tapped on it, a hologram popped out from the watch with the following text: Hello. Is anyone there? We are just passing through. We need rest.

Missy swiped away the hologram and gritted her teeth. She had dealt with people were "just passing through" and they almost killed her. She didn't respond, but waited.

Her watch indicated a knock on the door. Missy looked at the door, it was double locked with two deadbolts. Whoever lived here before made sure this place was security tight. There was only one window and one door- no other way for someone to intrude.

The hologram popped up with more text: Please, we mean no harm. It's hot. We have a child.

Missy sighed. She couldn't tell if they were being serious. If she denied the family and they were found dead later on, she knew the guilt would be unbearable. But these were mad times and only the fittest could survive. It wouldn't be her fault if they could not.

The hologram popped up, again: Please. Just some water for our daughter, that is all.

Missy clenched her teeth and closed her eyes tightly. She couldn't believe she was going against everything she learned.

Holding onto her shotgun close she unlocked the deadbolts and slowly opened the door.

She raised her barrel to face whoever was standing at the door.

A little girl was staring right inside the barrel with her two parents behind her. They were a young couple, probably not more than twenty-five, their brown faces covered with dirt and their clothing ripped. The only clean "thing" was their daughter, who barely had a speck of dirt on her.

They used everything they had for her, Missy thought.

Missy gestured for them to come in.

Her watch's hologram relayed the texts as the woman spoke.

"Thank you so much, we just walked for two days and we ran out of water. I saw your tank outside and it would be great if we could just take a couple bottles before we continue."

Missy put her hand up to allow the text to catch up with the speech. She finished reading and nodded.

The man looked puzzled at his wife.

"Can she speak English?"

Missy read that question on her watch and chuckled. Missy signed the international sign for "I'm Deaf" to the man.

Missy pressed a few buttons on her watch to change functions.

"I am deaf. I can communicate through the watch. Please take some water, but you have to leave right after." The watch spoke as Missy signed.

Missy stood by the unlocked door and watched as the couple quickly filled the water bottles up and placed them in their backpacks.

The little girl stood quietly and stared at her surroundings. Her deep brown eyes scrutinized every little detail. Her long black hair fell in waves just below her shoulders.

"What is your name?" Missy asked the girl.

"Sabrina," The little girl responded meekly.

"Very pretty name. Do you want to know how to sign it?"

Sabrina nodded. Missy fingerspelled all the letters and Sabrina copied.

Sabrina's parents watched as the interaction went on.

"How long have you been here?" The woman asked.

"A few months. I found this place empty. I was very lucky," Missy responded. She was looking at her watch for the time. They'd already been here too long. "I'm sorry, but you have to leave. I've survived this long because I've been on my own."

The couple nodded and agreed to leave. Sabrina waved goodbye to Missy as they walked out the door.

The woman stopped and turned before she walked out.

"We are forever in your debt..." The woman trailed off, waiting for a name.

"Missy."

"Missy, thank you."

"Wait. Don't go north. Okay? Bad people live north of here," Missy relayed the warning.

The couple nodded and they each took Sabrina's hands before heading west. Just like that, the family left. Missy was alone again.

She wondered if they would survive, wondered where they were headed. They said they've been walking for two days... where were they before?

Since the war broke out three years ago, this country's been destroyed. Anyone who could afford to leave the country, left. The others were left behind to deal with the aftermath.

Her parents died by the hands of the ex-military. They called themselves the *Cleaners*. They wanted to clean out anyone who wasn't "pure" enough to rebuild this country.

Missy looked down at her hands. They were getting paler. She hasn't been in the sunlight for days since she saw the Cleaners flag posted in the north. She was surprised they hadn't made their way to her yet.

She stared at her reflection on her watch. Her face was a dead giveaway that she wasn't "pure" in the sense of the Cleaners. She had slanted brown eyes, jet-black hair, and on top of that, she was deaf.

Missy spent the rest of the day eating canned soup and reading the same book she's read since the war broke. It was the only thing she was able to keep from her home when her parents tried to escape the regime.

The night her parents died, her mother told her to stay quiet and whatever she saw, to not come out until it was safe. Her mother gave Missy the smart watch and told her this would protect her. Missy was confused because up until recently it was just a smart watch. It wasn't anything special.

It wasn't until the Cleaners came to their hideout when she found out what her mom did to it. Her mom, the computer engineer and software designer for the company that made this watch, redesigned the interface so that it allowed Missy to be able to hear what was happening around her.

That hour Missy had held back her tears as she read what was happening around her. There was a lot of screaming; someone was barking orders, and then finally two gunshots.

She saw two bodies hit the floor through her blurred vision.

A couple pairs of feet walked around the place before they finally left. Missy crawled out after a few minutes to where her parents were.

Her dad was already gone; his soulless eyes stared blankly at the ceiling.

Her mom woke up briefly.

"My bag... security... take with you... run... hide..." Her mom was able to sign weakly. She took a shallow breath before closing her eyes. The last thing her mom signed was "I love you."

Missy wanted to scream. She was only a teenager. She wasn't prepared for this life. She ignored every single survival tactic lessons her school tried to teach the students before the teachers were banned. She didn't think anything bad could happen to them. People would put a stop to all the hatred before this got out of hand, she'd thought.

She was naïve.

When the Cleaners took out the headquarters of the ACLU and publicly executed every single lawyer that worked inside that was when her parents realized it wasn't safe. But by then, all flights outside of the country were grounded. People were banned from *leaving*.

Then Canada tried to help by bombing certain areas where the Cleaners were coordinating their efforts... but they ended up bombing civilians, too. They stopped that attack immediately, fearing any more unnecessary casualties. Other countries would not step in to help, since our country broke all alliances in the years prior.

The people were stuck. They were alone and left to die.

Missy was angry at the world for not stepping in. How could they let an entire population die? *Were we all expendable to them? Were we not significant enough to live?*

She promised herself that she would survive this so the future generations would know what happened here. She would do whatever it took to make sure the world couldn't forget what they ignored.

The light had gone down for the day. Missy walked around the shack, making sure the door was double locked and the window was tightly shut.

She crawled into her makeshift bed with her shotgun by her side and closed her eyes. She was running out of food, she reminded herself. She would have to wake up before dawn to get supplies.

Missy reset her alarm and went to sleep.

***

Walking to the local store was scary. Her watch kept vibrating at every single noise. She was getting jumpy. She walked stealthily with her shotgun clutched in her hands, finger ready on the trigger. She swiftly checked her surroundings from side to side.

Her drawstring bag hung tightly against her back. She only carried the essentials just in case she needed to set up camp somewhere else: the security alarms and her book.

The town was eerily devoid of humans. A lot of animals rummaged through trash and looted stores, but there were no signs of humanity. The animals seemed to not notice Missy, or not care about her as she walked past them in the aisles. All she needed was some more canned food. Her hot plate worked well enough to be able to eat comfortably.

As she turned to the canned food aisle, she gasped. It was empty. Others had the same idea.

In fact, the bloodied bodies on the ground showed just how far people would go.

One can remained, in the hand of the deceased. Missy slowly approached the body and tore the can out of its hand. She took a closer look and noticed the clothes looked familiar.

She took a few steps back when she realized... this was the couple she had saw that day... but there were only two bodies.

"Missy?" The voice triggered Missy's watch. She looked down and then looked around to find who spoke.

Missy signed, "Sabrina?"

Sabrina ran out from behind a bunch of boxes and hugged Missy tightly. Her little face was covered in snot and tears.

"Mama and Papa!" Sabrina cried.

"Shh." Missy was able to make that noise. "Sabrina, we have to be quiet. We don't want them coming back."

Sabrina nodded. She took Missy's hand and brought her to the boxes. The backpack that her father was carrying was hidden there.

She pointed at the bag and then pointed at Missy.

Missy understood that she was supposed to take the bag. She placed her own bag inside it before putting it on her back and grabbed Sabrina's hand.

Just like that, Missy wasn't alone anymore.

"Stay close to me. Run when I tell you. Okay?"

Sabrina nodded.

Together Missy and Sabrina walked out of the store quietly. Missy, still holding onto her shotgun tightly guided Sabrina back towards her shack. She felt her adrenaline pumping through her veins. She hadn't felt this much anxiety in a long time.

Her watch vibrated, Missy looked and Sabrina was whimpering. Missy gritted her teeth and kept inching forward. She needed to get to the shack now.

She didn't know until it was too late. A car revved up behind them and shined a bright light on them. Sabrina screamed.

Missy turned and faced the light with her shotgun. She was prepared to shoot anyone. It wouldn't be her first time.

Her watch vibrated and the hologram popped up: Lower that gun if you want to survive.

Sabrina looked up at Missy and grabbed on to her shirt. She tugged softly.

Missy signed, "Why would I do that? You could kill us."

The light shut off. It's completely dark. Missy took a step back, and brought the gun back up to her eyesight, waited.

Sabrina latched on to Missy's leg.

Missy looked at her watch for any sign of speech.

"Don't be afraid, we're a part of the resistance. We'll protect you." Her hologram wrote out.

Missy hesitated on lowering the gun.

A softer light shined in between them. There was a woman standing with her arms stretched out to show she was coming in peace. She started to sign.

"I used to be a teacher."

"All the teachers were killed."

"Not all." The woman gestured behind her and four others stepped out of the SUV. "We went underground before they started killing... We just won back this area from the Cleaners and we were looking for survivors to take back."

"They killed her parents. She needs someone to look after her. I won't be able to."

"You can come with us too." The woman encouraged.

"It's better to travel in low numbers. Groups become easy targets." Missy shook her head.

"You won't have to travel anymore, I promise. We have a school building set up for all the survivors."

Missy hesitated.

Sabrina looked up at her and shook her head, "I'm not going without you."

Missy wanted to trust these people. She really did. But there were so many times she came across a group of people who claimed they were "part of the resistance" and ended up being worse that the Cleaners. But the woman said they were teachers.

"You have to make your decision now. We have to leave," The woman signed hastily.

Sabrina reached and tugged on Missy's shirt again. It was her way of reassuring Missy.

Missy lowered her gun and walked to the woman. The woman smiled.

"I'm Carrie."

"Missy."

Missy and Sabrina piled into the SUV and they were hauled away... far from where they first met.

When the sun finally rose, the SUV approached a huge brick building. It looked more like an old warehouse than a school.

Sabrina stared out the window excitedly for she just spotted a playground with a few children playing on it.

The SUV pulled in through the security gates and brought the occupants to the front door. When it stopped, Carrie hopped out and met with another woman who exited the building.

The door opened for Missy and Sabrina to disembark out of the car. Missy held onto

Sabrina protectively, which was weird because she only just met her yesterday.

The new woman stood in front of them with a huge welcoming smile. Her long black hair mirrored Sabrina's. Missy thought it was uncanny.

Sabrina's eyes lit up and she ran to the woman to give her a huge hug.

"Auntie Naomi!" Sabrina started crying. Naomi scooped up Sabrina and squeezed her tight.

"I was so worried." Naomi kissed Sabrina on the top of her head. "You're safe now, *mija*."

Naomi looked at Sabrina with sorrow-filled eyes and then noticed Missy.

"Welcome. My name is Naomi. We don't quite have a name for this place yet, but we've been calling ourselves the sanctuary. Come on and we can get you settled."

Carrie attempted to interpret, but Missy showed her that her watch was captioning their conversation.

Carrie found it intriguing and while they walked into the building she inquired about everything the watch did. Missy explained that her mother made everything.

"She was a very intelligent woman. I learned almost everything I know from her." Missy looked down at her feet, then back at Carrie. "She was my best friend."

Carrie nodded and took Missy in for a hug. At first, Missy wanted to reject the hug, but as the feeling of safety washed over her, she didn't want to let go.

"She is still with you, Missy. This watch proves it." Carrie tapped Missy's wrist. "Come, you'll want to see this."

Carrie and Missy caught up with Naomi and Sabrina. Naomi led Missy and Sabrina into the common room. It was filled with families, children, and people Missy's age. The one thing that Missy found astounding was the amount of color she saw on everyone. Latinx, Black, and Asian faces stared back at Missy. A tear escaped her eye.

And just like that, Missy will never be alone.

ZOE

4/18/18

DEAR DIARY,

   I don't know where I belong. There are two worlds where I half fit in.

   Hearing.

   Deaf.

   I met a deaf person today at the coffee shop. We were set up on a blind date. It was the first time I ever met anyone who was just like me. He wore hearing aids and spoke, but he also used sign language to communicate. I never learned sign language.

He laughed at me. How could I be deaf and not know sign language? He was baffled. I became embarrassed and I yelled at him for being rude and ran off.

I hope I never run into him again. I'm embarrassed for myself that I yelled at him. I'm embarrassed that I didn't know sign language.

I realized then, I didn't really fit in the deaf world.

But today also reminded me that I didn't fit in the hearing world either. I went to meet my friends for drinks after the horrible coffee date. They decided on this noisy bar and I couldn't hear any of them when they spoke. It was hard. I kept asking them what they said and it became apparent that it was getting annoying.

I wanted to cry, but I didn't. I stopped asking them questions and I sat back and just watched everyone interact with each other. They laughed, I tried to laugh along with them, but I didn't know what they were laughing about.

So where do I belong?

I feel like I'm stuck in the middle of two gigantic worlds and no one would fully accept me. I had one hand in the Deaf world and the other in the Hearing world but no one will reach out and pull me into either.

I feel alone. I thought that maybe the blind date I met for coffee would understand my loneliness, but deaf parents raised him. He was already a part of *that* world.

My parents were great at raising me and making sure I didn't feel any different, but they'll never understand that identity crisis I am going through. They don't have that "disability" that set them apart from their peers. They'll never have to question if someone will accept them. They've already been accepted.

Who am I?

I don't know if I can answer that question. I hope I can find out soon.

Yours truly,
Zoe

6/20/18

Dear Diary,

Emi Sano

Am I too old to have a diary? This feels silly to want to write in a diary, but I feel like I have no one to talk to that understands me.

Anyway, I met a guy. He is everything I ever wanted in a boyfriend. It didn't even bother him that I was hard of hearing either. He thought it was pretty neat.

We've been dating for a few weeks now... and we're about to have our first "sleepover". I put them in quotes because we all know what happens when adults have sleepovers, don't we?

I'm nervous. Whenever I had a guy stay the night I've always slept with my hearing aids on in case they want to talk when we wake up, but I just got new hearing aids and they ring whenever I put my head on the pillow. I need to take them out in order to get some sleep. Will he still like me even though I can't hear him in the morning?

Will he think I'm ignoring him as we fall asleep?

Unfortunately these questions have to be asked... those were one of the reasons why my past boyfriends broke up with me.

It was too weird for them to be dating a "deaf" girl.

He's coming over in a couple hours. Wish me luck.

Yours truly,
Zoe

6/21/18

Dear Diary,

Sleepover was a success! He was patient with me when we woke up and waited for me to put in my hearing aids to talk. I feel like I found someone who truly accepts me. I'm over the moon right now.

That's all.

Yours truly,
Zoe

7/6/18

Dear Diary,

I think we're going to break up soon. I could see the frustration on his face today when

Emi Sano

I kept asking him what his friends were saying at the bar we went to.

"Don't worry about it."

"It's not important."

He started to ignore me towards the end of the night.

I went home without him.

I don't know how to fix me.

How do I make it so I don't lose another boyfriend?

Yours truly,

Zoe

7/15/18

Dear Diary,

We didn't break up.

I told him how I felt at the bar and he apologized. He said he didn't realize how much it hurt me and how I felt pushed out of the group. He promised that the next time we all hang out it'd be in a less noisy place.

I still feel a little broken inside, but I'm glad he understands now.

I just hope it sticks.

226

It kind of reminded me of the time when I was in high school and my parents would have to come into a meeting with my teachers to remind them that I needed written notes for oral lectures or closed captioning for movies. The teachers always apologized, claimed they'd change, and then do so for two weeks before returning back to their old way.

I hope he isn't going to be like my teachers, but we'll see.

Yours truly,
Zoe

8/2/18

Dear Diary,
We are still having communication issues. I'm so frustrated with him now. I thought things would change. I thought he understood. I don't know what else to do.

Tonight we had a huge argument. I'm crying as I write. He kept saying I was overreacting.

He called me a drama queen before I left his place.

Emi Sano

I want to stop crying. I just want to find someone who understands me. I thought he would be the one to.

I texted my friends; they're coming over to talk. One of them is bringing wine. Hopefully I'll feel better.

Yours truly,

Zoe

10/4/18

Dear Diary,

I broke up with him.

I gave him three more months to change, but he kept going back to the way he was the first time at the bar. He would always ignore me after several questions.

Before I left him he claimed he would be better. He swore he loved me.

It hurt because I loved him, too.

But I knew he didn't love all of me. He didn't love my deaf part. That will always be a part of me.

Once again, I'm alone.

Yours truly,

Zoe

11/29/18

Dear Diary,

I ran into that coffee date guy again. The one who laughed at me because I didn't know sign language? He apologized... a lot. He told me how bad he felt after I cursed him out and ran off.

I don't remember cursing him out but he smirked when I tried to say I didn't.

He also told me that my coworker that set us up chewed him out for days afterwards.

He asked me if he could have a second chance. I didn't know if I should, but I've been having bad luck with hearing men that maybe if I dated a deaf man, it'd be different.

He taught me some signs.

I only remember how to sign "thank you" and "happy".

This was the first time I've smiled since my last break up.

I hope it doesn't go away.

Yours truly,

Emi Sano

Zoe

12/2/19

Dear Diary,

It's been awhile. I was reading over what I wrote in the past and man, did I have an identity crisis. I'm better now. I've been dating the coffee date guy for a year now. I guess I've been just using this diary as a place to vent, instead of a place to put down memories. I'm hoping this entry will change that.

I finally feel like I've been accepted, but not to one world. I've finally accepted myself into both worlds. I learned that I could live in both simultaneously. I didn't need to be a part of just one. My boyfriend taught me that.

I'm so grateful I gave him a second chance.

Oh and I know a ton of more signs now. We can have conversations in sign language. I feel like we're little kids talking in our secret language whenever we're out in public. It's so much fun.

We're going out for our anniversary date tonight... is it bad that I hope he proposes?

Yours truly,
Zoe

P.S. HE DID.

Acknowledgements

Thank you to my wonderful family and friends who have supported me on my writing journey. Mom, Dad, Grammie, Mieko, Joseph, Liz, Corinne, Marissa, Sara, Emily P., Odessa, Monze, Omar, Michaela, Oscar, Emily L., and all the writers in social media communities.

None of this would have been possible if it weren't for your help with emotional support, reading, becoming a patron, career/life decision-making, and giving me advice on writing and self-publishing. Without your support, I wouldn't be where I am today.

And lastly thank you, dear reader, for taking the time to read my short stories. I hope you enjoyed them as much as I enjoyed writing.

About the Author

Emi Sano grew up in a small town of New Hampshire and studied Film at Rochester Institute of Technology where she crafted her storytelling in the form of scriptwriting. Emi has worked in the film industry as a screenwriter and script supervisor. Her writing career took off after she started a writing blog [writingcreatingmagic.com] where she would post short stories.

The stories she writes and chooses to work on are mainly about real life dramas, but she isn't afraid to dabble in fantasy/folklore every now and then.

Emi Sano

Emi enjoys her time with her family, whether it is exploring the nature around her in North Carolina or in the comfort of home.

"Voices" is her debut published work.

COMING SOON

WE DON'T TALK ABOUT THAT
a novella

Kevin was awake with his anxiety levels mellowed, hallucinations subsided, but it didn't stop his thoughts. How could she hate me so much? He thought to himself, what did I do to deserve this? Why me? He was trapped in a prison cell that was his own mind.

Kevin and Molly have two views about their parents.

Kevin, a diagnosed schizophrenic, thinks his parents believe he's damaged goods. Molly, an overachieving honor student, understands her parents want what's best for them. After Kevin's suicide attempt, Molly starts to view their family the way Kevin had and forces her parents to see the damage they have caused.

My mother turned to us and said, "Not a word about this to anyone."

Emi Sano

I looked at my dad, he agreed. I didn't.
In We Don't Talk About, we explore what life is like in a home of a young Asian American teenager struggling to cope with schizophrenia and what happens to the family after a suicide attempt becomes the final rip that tears them apart.

Coming to you September 2019!